Mobile

DEMCO

CAMERON
CASTLE

Also by Marilyn Ross
in Large Print:

Message from a Ghost

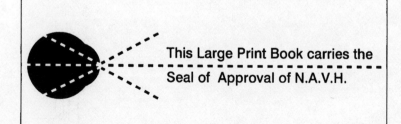

This Large Print Book carries the
Seal of Approval of N.A.V.H.

CAMERON CASTLE

Marilyn Ross

Thorndike Press • Waterville, Maine

Published in 2002 by arrangement with
Maureen Moran Agency.

Thorndike Press Large Print Candlelight Series.

The tree indicium is a trademark of Thorndike Press.

The text of this Large Print edition is unabridged.
Other aspects of the book may vary from the original edition.

Set in 16 pt. Plantin.

Printed in the United States on permanent paper.

Library of Congress Cataloging-in-Publication Data

Ross, Marilyn, 1912–
    Cameron Castle / Marilyn Ross.
        p. cm.
    ISBN 0-7862-4608-1 (lg. print : hc : alk. paper)
    1. Inheritance and succession — Fiction. 2. Married
women — Fiction. 3. Nova Scotia — Fiction. I. Title.
PR9199.3.R5996 C36 2002
    813′.54—dc21
                                                    2002026605

To Susan and Joel Jacobson

CHAPTER ONE

The gray clouds had first gathered as she'd come down the landing steps of the sleek jet, which had brought her in less than two hours from her native Boston to Halifax in northeastern Canada. A bride of only a few days, Laura Cameron had worried that this introduction to the foreign land in which she would be making her home might be considered an omen. An ill omen.

The wind, that early day in May, had been bitterly cold, and she had drawn her cloth coat with its heavy fur collar closely about her. Donald, her new husband, had warned her the weather would be more rugged in Nova Scotia and so she had been persuaded to wear the brown tweed coat. The cold and the cloudy skies had combined to give her a pang of homesickness and a feeling of uneasiness.

She had turned to glance back at her husband and found scant hint of understanding in the solemn face of the tall, dark-haired man to whom she'd so recently entrusted her future. She had always been led to think that Scotch people had dour, withdrawn dispositions, but she had never noticed this in Donald Cameron until after their marriage. Until then he had been an amusing, carefree companion not noticeably different from the other Boston young men whom she had dated. But within twenty-four hours after the wedding this weird transformation had taken place in him. She could not decide whether it had shown first when he'd received the wire from home, the wire he would not let her see, or if it had started at the modest wedding reception at the Sheraton-Plaza Hotel when her Aunt Alice had reprimanded him for taking her back to Canada so soon. She hadn't blamed Donald for resenting her Aunt's comment and knew that the older woman had merely used this as an excuse to vent her wrath on him. She didn't like him.

Laura's brief glimpse of her husband, as she had looked over her shoulder at him on the landing steps, had made her wonder uneasily if her Aunt Alice might have been close to the truth when she had dubbed him a tightfisted, dour opportunist, ready to marry any American girl with enough money who would have him. Of course this had been the bitter opinion of a spinster losing her favorite niece and it had been completely unfair to Donald to even have thought it.

So she had pushed the nagging doubt out of her mind on the four-hour bus trip that took them from the gray, old, fortress city of Halifax to the highlands of Cape Breton — the Scotland of the North American continent. Laura had heard so much about it that she had found herself eagerly staring out the bus window at the rugged, rural country. Its ribbon of a road winding high in the hills and skirting the cliffs with the white beaches far below. A land of evergreens, great rocks and the blue sea.

Donald had become more like his former self on the bus trip, pointing out places of interest along the way and telling her how long it would be before they would reach the town of Glengarry and Cameron Castle. It had thrilled her to think she would actually be living in a castle more than a hundred years old, and she had looked forward to her first view of it with growing anticipation. Donald's sensitive, handsome face had glowed as he told her about it, and she had begun to think that all would be well again.

Glengarry had turned out to be a cluster

of gray, frame wood houses along a main street and little more. There were a few stores, and a post office which also served as a bus stop. It was there that Graham, the estate manager, had met them. He was a man about Donald's size and age, with a sandy complexion and the same solemn cast of countenance. When they were introduced he had shown a minimum of enthusiasm and had quickly gathered their bags, put them in the trunk of the car and chauffeured them along the narrow, paved road that twisted its way up the coast to Cameron Castle.

Now she stood on the lawn outside the impressive stone building with its forbidding gray towers and ivy-covered wings. Its very size and bleak appearance served to make her feel more insecure. She did not feel equal to being the mistress of such a mansion. It was close to five hours since she had set foot in Canada at the distant airport of Halifax. All during that time the sun had been blotted out by the grim array of clouds, and Donald's handsome, young face had been almost as grim as the afternoon.

She was certain that he loved her. His embraces and kisses had not lessened in their ardor, but she felt that something was worrying him. She determined to find out what it was at the first opportunity and settle this uneasiness between them.

For the moment, however, she was occupied by her introduction to Cameron Castle. Graham had vanished as soon as he had taken in their bags and, while Donald kept her in the great, shadowed reception hall, he filled in the time by telling her of the history of the old mansion.

"My great-grandfather built it in 1860," he told her with pride. "He came to Canada with the great influx from Scotland after the Highland troubles. The period when greedy landlords dispossessed their tenant farmers and after burning their homes, drove them off the land overnight."

"But why?" Laura asked, shocked at this revelation of the dark days in Scotland's past.

"A lust for money," Donald told her grimly. "They wanted to use the land for giant herds of sheep. In the end it proved a failure and most of the area reverted to wild game. Even today many estates over there have private game preserves on what was once tenant acreage."

She listened to his account of those past days with interest, speculating that he must have some special reason for keeping her in the entrance hall rather than taking her directly upstairs to their room.

He broke into her reverie by saying, "My grandfather did not come to this country a poor man. But he could not stand the goings-on in his area of Scotland at that time. He decided to come out here with the immigrants and build a home and a model community. So Glengarry was born and this house soon became a landmark of the countryside."

She sighed. "It is impressive."

A smile played at the corners of his mouth. "And run-down and in need of almost everything to make it decently modern," he said. "I'm afraid you've arrived too late to see the great days of the Camerons!"

"Who speaks of the great days of the Camerons?" a majestic female voice inquired. Laura turned quickly to the winding steps that led from above and saw a fantastic yet striking figure slowly descending the stairway.

"Aunt Caroline!" Donald exclaimed and stepped across to meet her.

The old woman was tall, with a long, severe face and large blue eyes that glittered with brightness in the ravaged countenance. Her gray hair was combed in a high upsweep, which made her seem to tower above them. A black woolen shawl was draped across her shoulders over an austere, dark brown dress with a high collar and which flowed down almost touching the ground. She had a cameo at her throat and leaned heavily on a black, silver-headed cane for support.

As Donald led her forward to meet Laura, the old woman asked, "What about the welcoming ceremony? Where is Graham? Must he always be late!"

"He'll be along in a moment," Donald said placatingly. "Aunt Caroline, this is Laura."

The old woman turned her bright gaze on her and with a smile said, "Welcome to Cameron Castle, Laura. Kiss me, child!"

Laura felt that here was a friend. She went forward to the old woman, whom she knew must be eighty or more, and touched her lips to the dry, wrinkled cheek.

"Donald has told me about you, Aunt Caroline."

The blue eyes regarded her. "I expect he has," she said. "I'm much nicer than he has painted me."

"I did nothing but flatter you," Donald protested, amused at her comment.

She nodded absently and stared at Laura again. "She is pretty. No one could deny that. But there have been pretty ones before and it did them no good in this house." She paused. "She's nothing but a *bairn!*"

Laura felt herself blushing at this Scots reference to her being a child. A child at twenty-three! Impulsively she burst out, "I'm twenty-three, Aunt Caroline, and that's far from being a youngster!"

Donald put his arm around Laura protectively. "That's the truth," he said. And with an affectionate glance down at her, he went on. "Twenty-three, blonde and with the oval face of an angel. A pert, healthy angel, I'll admit, and she's a fine horsewoman and has a figure that does more than justice to her riding habit."

Aunt Caroline appeared to have lost interest. She glanced around irritably. "What has happened to Graham?" she demanded. "I declare, I don't see why you keep him on. You know your father won't like this being kept waiting!"

Laura looked up at Donald with startled eyes. She knew that his father had long been dead and for a moment this reference to him shocked her. Donald gave her a warning glance and then she remembered.

He had prepared her for this back in Boston, explaining that his elderly aunt's mind sometimes wandered and it was not unusual for her to refer to the dead as if they were still part of her world.

The awkward moment ended when Graham made his appearance along the hallway that apparently led directly to the rear of the mansion. But it was a different Graham from the reticent chauffeur who had driven them from Glengarry. He was now in red plaid kilts, a dark blue jacket with brass buttons and a jaunty, blue Scots cap with tails down the back. He carried a set of bagpipes.

Donald smiled at Laura. "This is what we've been waiting for," he told her. "I wanted you to have a traditional welcome to Cameron Castle."

"Well, hurry up with it, Graham," Aunt Caroline said querulously. "We've been waiting endlessly for you!"

Graham's solemn young face turned red as he stood holding the door open for the other three to file out. Laura felt sympathy for the young estate manager, caught between the old woman's impatience and Donald's wish to have him provide a colorful touch for her arrival.

Graham hurried ahead as soon as they

were all outside and made his way across the lawn to the flagpole on which flew a Union Jack. Laura knew that Canada had a flag of its own with a maple leaf in red. But she was also aware that those with strong affection for the Old Country refused to give up the red, white and blue that marked an outpost of Britain wherever it was raised. Apparently Donald was one of the loyalists.

Aunt Caroline hobbled ahead, moving vigorously with the aid of her cane and the black shawl clutched around her for protection. Donald and Laura followed a short distance behind. They all took a stand about twenty feet from Graham, who was now directly below the flag. He lifted the pipes to his mouth and at once began to bring forth that combination of mournfulness and liveliness that is the peculiar music of the bagpipes.

Donald smiled down at her. "I wanted you to know you have arrived in Scots country," he said.

"It's wonderful," she told him, knowing it meant a great deal to him. And in a way it was stirring. The cold spring wind made the Union Jack flutter majestically as the music of the pipes built to a noble peak. Graham began to pace up and down in a one-man parade as he continued to play. Aunt Caroline listened in silence with an admiring smile on her ancient face.

Laura gazed beyond the piper and the flag at the evergreens on the slope below, leading down to the winding asphalt road that followed the coastline and whose white center strip stood out even in the dull gray of this forbidding afternoon. On the other side of the road was an area of more evergreens which gave way to gaunt cliffs. Below them were the beach and the everlasting stretch of Atlantic Ocean, broken only by a small island a far distance from the shore at this point. Cameron Castle and its grounds towered above the surrounding area. Donald's ancestor had chosen the spot well.

At last the bagpipes ended and Graham smiled their way. Laura at once clapped loudly and smiled at him in return. "Thank you, Graham," she called out. "It's a moment I'll never forget."

Donald had lost his grimness for the time being and looked pleased. "That is my hope," he said.

She placed a hand on his arm and looked up at him with gentle eyes. "It's a lovely spot. I know we're going to be happy here."

At once some of the concern returned to

his sensitive face. "I hope so," he said, almost as if he doubted it. Before she could make any comment on this, he took her arm. "I must take you to our room now. You're surely tired and will need time to freshen up before you meet the others at dinner."

Aunt Caroline had deserted them to cross the lawn and join Graham, with whom she lingered to have some private discussion. As Laura and Donald made their way back to the entrance of the gray stone mansion some scattered snowflakes began to drift idly down.

"Oh, no!" Laura protested. "Not snow! Not in May!"

He smiled. "It doesn't mean anything. We often get snow flurries until late in the month. But it's only once in years we ever have a real storm."

"I should hope so," she exclaimed as they entered the house.

He took her up the winding stairway and she saw that the first landing was nicely carpeted and several oil paintings of another era hung on its walls. It was actually dark but she imagined that at night, with the lights turned on, it could be quite pleasant. She also noticed a cold dampness in the house and guessed that it presented problems in heating. It had been built in the days when the standards of comfort had demanded much less warmth than in modern times. She gave a little shiver as they started up the second flight of stairs.

It brought them to another shadowed landing and Donald led her down a wide hallway whose light was derived from a window far down at its end. He paused at the second door on the right and threw it open.

"This is our room," he told her.

She entered hesitantly and looked around her. It was a large room with a high ceiling. The two windows overlooked the ocean since the room was located at the front of the house. The color scheme of the room was mainly crimson for which Laura was grateful. It gave it a feeling of much-needed warmth. Great crimson drapes hung at each window and the wide bed had a crimson coverlet. The walls were done with a crimson and gray patterned wallpaper, and the large fireplace was built of the same gray stone as the exterior of the mansion. A Persian rug, in suitable matching colors, covered most of the floor, and the furniture was ornate and had the quality of genuine antique design.

Opening a door on the right wall, she

discovered a large closet that was really a small room in itself, and further along was another door leading to a spacious bathroom with elaborate fixtures dating back at least fifty years. Yet it was spotlessly clean and appeared well-preserved in spite of its age.

As she returned from her tour of inspection, Donald looked at her anxiously. "You don't really think it is too bad?"

"Of course not," she said. "It's nice and it's interesting. How do you heat it?"

"There are forced hot air vents and occasionally the fireplace is used," he explained. Then he asked her, "Are you cold now?"

She shook her head. "I'll be fine as soon as I've had a warm bath and change for dinner."

He nodded and glanced at his wristwatch. "It took us longer to get here than we expected. You won't have much time to spare."

Laura looked around and saw the bags were all installed. "Graham didn't waste any time," she said. "No wonder he kept us waiting. He brought all our bags up and that will save me time now when I unpack."

"Good. You'll be meeting Mrs. Basset,

the housekeeper, later. Apparently she's out somewhere on an errand. She runs this place almost completely alone, you know."

"That must be a job!"

"It's not fair," he sighed. "But then we haven't much choice."

Laura came close to him and snuggled in his arms. "There is that shadowed look on your face again," she reproved him. "I've seen entirely too much of it these last few days."

"I'm sorry," he said.

"You do love me, don't you?" she asked, staring up into his serious face. "You aren't feeling you've made a mistake so soon?"

"Of course not. If I'd searched the world I couldn't have found a wife to suit me better than you," he said quietly. As if to prove his words, he bent down and kissed her.

She welcomed the touch of his lips to hers. It gave her some assurance at a moment when she badly needed it. She enjoyed the embrace for a long moment and when he released her she spoke of what was foremost in her mind.

"I'm your wife now, Donald," she said. "And I expect to share your worries. I know you've been bothered ever since you received that wire in Boston. I wish you'd tell me what was in it."

He at once retreated within himself, his face expressionless. "It had to do with business here. Nothing that you should be troubled with."

"I think I should be told anything that upsets you the way that news seemed to."

Donald turned toward the door. "Please don't think anything more about it," he said. "I'll be waiting for you downstairs." He paused in the doorway. "Be sure and look your prettiest." With a small smile he went out and closed the door behind him.

She stood staring in the direction of the door for a moment, somewhat forlorn. He had neatly gotten out of telling her anything, though she still was sure he was badly worried. It would have to wait until later and then she would try and question him again. In spite of his efforts to give her a traditional welcome at Cameron Castle, this was not a happy homecoming. His strange aloofness was marring the occasion.

After she had unpacked the bags Laura prepared to take a bath. She discovered then how ancient the plumbing in the old mansion really was. Only after an annoying period of waiting, of hearing pipes gurgle and groan, and of endlessly running cold water, did she get a sufficient supply of moderately warm water to take her bath. The house had been allowed to run down.

It brought back her Aunt Alice's warnings and dark premonitions. "You haven't known that young man nearly long enough to decide you want him for a husband!" she had insisted.

"I love Donald and how long we've known each other isn't important," Laura had argued.

Her aunt had paced restlessly before the divan on which she was seated. "And what is he? Some sort of musician from Canada! You know he must be penniless!"

"He's not a musician," Laura had said. "He's a composer and a good one. The Boston Symphony is going to play his 'Island Echoes' and he has plans to do a symphony one day."

Aunt Alice's pinched face had registered scorn. "One day!" she had scoffed. "And what, may I ask, is he living on now?"

"He has an estate in the highlands of Cape Breton," Laura had answered. "It has been in his family for years. He operates the farm with the help of a manager."

"Land-poor! Likely that's the story. Precious few of those estates pay in these days. Mark my words, young lady, this is no case of love at first sight! That young man is marrying you for your money!"

"But that's so unfair," Laura had protested. "My money is my money!"

"As long as you're alive," Aunt Alice had admitted grudgingly. "Providing he doesn't wheedle it out of you. And perhaps he is counting on being a widower and having it all."

"Aunt Alice!" Laura had stood up, aghast at the monstrous accusation.

The pinched face had shown uneasiness. "Well, if I were you I'd make a will before I went off to Canada with him. And I'd make the kind that wouldn't benefit him no matter what happened."

"I'll take care of that in my own way," Laura had said coldly as she left her aunt.

Stung by the way in which her aunt had talked, she had determined to show her confidence in Donald Cameron. She had even insisted that he accompany her to the office of her lawyer while she had dictated the change in her will. A change that gave all her fortune to him in the event of her death. Donald had seemed ill at ease and embarrassed and when they had left the lawyer's office he had argued with her.

"I wish you hadn't done that," he had said. "And I'm particularly unhappy that you let me know about it."

"I have a right to do what I like with my money," she'd told him with a smile. "Money never brings anyone happiness. Mine certainly hasn't for me. I don't consider it of that much importance. But I want you to have it if anything should happen to me."

It seemed that at least one portion of her aunt's prediction was coming true. If the state of Cameron Castle was any indication, it seemed fairly certain that her husband was in financial straits. Otherwise he would surely have done something to keep the fine old building in better repair. At once she began to think of some way she could offer him money for that purpose without hurting his feelings. She might present it to him as a desire on her part to redecorate much of the mansion and, in doing so, slyly arrange to have a lot of needed repairs done at the same time. She shivered as she got out of the bath. A new heating system would be one thing that would certainly benefit them all.

Finding the switch, she turned on the chandelier that hung from the middle of the ceiling and provided the room's only light. It was of old-fashioned crystal design and she guessed it might have held candles or lamps before being converted to electricity. Certainly the conversion had done little in the way of providing good light. She quickly drew the crimson drapes across the windows and seated herself at the dressing table with its big oval mirror and low top. The mirror was a good one, but she still had trouble making up because of the poor light.

She decided it might be wise to wear something warm and selected a two-piece woolen suit in robin's egg blue and a white blouse. She felt more comfortable with it on and hoped that Donald would approve. With a final glimpse in the mirror, she brushed a lock of unruly blonde hair in place and then hurried to the door.

The lights were on in the hallways and although the bulbs were of low wattage and the wall brackets a long distance apart, they did serve to give the old house a more comfortable air. She hesitated slightly as she began her descent of the last stairway, aware of voices coming from the living room. She quickly went over all who lived in the mansion and their relationship to her husband. Aside from Caroline, who was actually his great-aunt, there was his father's brother, a philosophy professor at Dunwood College situated about twenty miles away. His name was Austin Cameron and he was a widower with one grown stepdaughter, Anna Gordon. Donald had spoken little of the girl except to mention that she was a teacher at the local school. She knew that Donald had a brother, Frank, who was a lawyer. But he did not live in the house, having a cottage of his own which he shared with his invalid wife. Laura doubted that Frank would be on hand for dinner since Donald had mentioned that his wife had recently taken a turn for the worse. She suffered from some obscure form of anaemia.

Deciding she must face whomever might be there, she made her way down the rest of the stairs and moved across the reception hall to the double doors of the large living room. Only one or two table lamps were lit to break the shadows that filled the big room, along with the glow that came from a log fire in the great stone fireplace. Donald was standing in silhouette with his back to the blazing logs. At his right stood a stout, balding man with a round pleasant face, and in an easy chair across from them was a startlingly lovely brunette.

Donald, looking proud and pleased, came down the length of the room to meet her with outstretched hands. "You didn't keep us waiting after all," he said. "Come and meet the others."

Professor Austin Cameron held her hand for a moment longer than was comfortable. "We must be good friends," he said. "I understand you are interested in books. They are my life."

She smiled, feeling awkward as his moist hand continued to clutch hers. "I'll look forward to a long discussion on the subject," she said.

Donald then directed her to Anna, who had risen from her chair. The dark girl had large, luminous eyes that now searched Laura carefully. "You're as attractive as Donald said you were," was her quiet compliment.

"Too bad the weather wasn't better for your arrival," Austin Cameron said briskly. "It can be nice this time of year. And it soon will be, at any rate."

"Don't try to deceive Laura about the climate here," Anna said with dry humor. "She'll find out the sad truth soon enough." To her directly she added, "It's a rugged country in every way."

"We draw our strength from that," Donald said. "I wouldn't trade this spot for any other in the world."

His Uncle Austin chuckled. "We know

how you feel about it, Donald. No need to go into details."

They talked for a few minutes about the estate and Austin Cameron told her about his college and that it was the only one in North America that held a summer seminar in Gaelic, the ancient language of the Scots that dates back to before the Norman invasion of England.

"Is Gaelic actually a living language here?" she asked.

"Indeed it is," Austin said. "At the college we teach piping and other Highland lores as well, and every year it's the scene of the annual Gaelic Mod."

"Gaelic Mod?" Laura was puzzled.

"A festival of the arts," Anna informed her. "With the emphasis on games and music as well. We have a similar thing here on the estate every June, but we call it a Highland Gathering."

"And it's only weeks away," Donald said. "There are a great many preparations to be looked after still. Many letters to be written and mailed." He smiled at Laura. "That's a job you can help me with this year."

At this point Aunt Caroline made her usual impressive entrance. She refused to lean on the offered arm of Austin

Cameron and instead advanced regally on her own, to seat herself in the easy chair closest to the blazing logs.

There, leaning on her cane, she motioned for Laura to come and be seated on the footstool near her. Laura obeyed as Donald went to the sideboard to pour wine for them all. Anna moved over to assist him in serving and Austin retreated to a spot beside the fireplace, leaving Laura comparatively isolated with the old lady.

Aunt Caroline was wearing a black lace gown in the same style as the dress Laura had seen her in that afternoon. Now a silver ornament graced her throat, twinkling with a dancing pattern from the red, blue and yellow flames of the logs reflecting on it. The bright, old eyes fastened on Laura.

"Too pretty for her own good," she said to no one in particular.

"I hope we'll be good friends," Laura said. "You know this country so well. You can be such a help to me in explaining things."

"Aye." The wrinkled face showed a faint smile. "That I can do." She rested thin, blue-veined hands on the silver head of the cane. "So you won Donald after all. I didn't think it could happen."

Laura's eyebrows raised. "Why not?"

Aunt Caroline stared at the flames. "Donald has always loved this land and little else. This house is his temple of worship. No one else would have held on to it as he has. It's his true mistress."

She gazed around the big living room with its old but rich furnishings, at the paintings on the walls and the ornaments and silver that decorated the tables and sideboard. "It is a lovely old place," she agreed. "I think I understand his love for it."

Aunt Caroline chuckled. "You have a rival, my dear. Be careful of Sheila MacLeod. 'Tis she, I suspect, who holds the key to Donald's heart."

The old woman's words came as a shock. Laura could scarcely believe what she had heard. Aunt Caroline was calmly telling her that there was another woman in Donald's life. Could that explain the wire and his strange behavior since?

Anna came with wine for her and Aunt Caroline. Austin moved close to chat over his wine glass with Aunt Caroline, and Laura got up and took a step away to stand by Anna. Donald had left the room for a moment.

Laura offered the girl a forlorn smile.

31

"Aunt Caroline has surprised me. She says I have a rival for Donald's affections. A Sheila MacLeod!"

Anna nodded. "You have. But don't worry. She's been dead a hundred years."

CHAPTER TWO

Anna's casual statement had an even more surprising effect on Laura. She stared at her. "Sheila MacLeod has been dead a hundred years!"

"A little more actually," Anna said with a thin smile showing on her lovely face. "Her death dates back to the building of Cameron Castle."

"But I don't understand!"

"The connection between the long dead Sheila and your husband?" Anna asked lightly. "It's really quite simple if you think of it the way Aunt Caroline does."

Laura glanced at the old woman who was now in earnest conversation with Austin Cameron and then again at Anna. She said, "I know she has a habit of confusing the dead with the living. Donald warned me."

"It does get a bit disconcerting at times," Anna agreed and took a sip of her wine. "But in this case she isn't mixed up. She was using Sheila MacLeod as a symbolic figure to represent the castle. She meant that Donald is obsessed with this old house and keeping it in his possession. And that hasn't been easy. It seems each year the estate goes further in debt."

"I didn't know that," Laura admitted.

"It's true," Anna said, glancing around at the big, shadow-filled room. "My father stays on here because he likes his position at the college and enjoys the Gaelic and the country. I stay because he is here and I haven't any better sense. Both of us contribute rental and board money to Donald, probably more than we'd pay anywhere else. So does Aunt Caroline from her small allowance. We've all joined with him in a futile attempt to keep the castle in the family."

"Why do you say futile?"

Anna shrugged. "Because I believe he will lose it in the end, and that worries me. Donald is a very sensitive person, who until he met you has known happiness only in this place and in his music. I dislike thinking what losing the estate will do to him."

Laura frowned. "Then we mustn't let that happen!"

It was Anna's turn to be surprised. "You can help prevent it?"

"I think so," she said quietly.

Anna studied her mockingly. "How lucky Donald was to meet someone like you," she murmured, a soft meaningful note in her voice. She took another sip from her wine glass.

Laura thought she knew what Anna meant. She was making the same accusation that Aunt Alice had made back in Boston — suggesting that Donald had married her only for her money, and she resented it as bitterly as she had when it came from her aunt. Yet she didn't want to begin her stay at the mansion by having words with the girl.

In an effort to turn the conversation into other channels, she asked, "What is the story about Sheila MacLeod? The name fascinates me."

Anna smiled. "Every big house in this part of the world has its ghost. Highlanders are a mystic lot and we Cape Bretoners are no exception. The creatures of the mist and night are all too familiar to us. Sheila MacLeod is the ghost of Cameron Castle. In Glengarry folk whisper that on certain nights she can be seen from afar, moving from one turret to another. Her ghostly form outlined against the darkness."

"A legend of the district, I suppose."

"With a basis in fact. It is said she walks in the corridors of the house as well. A pretty, young girl in a flowing white gown, with long silver hair and a winsome face. A lovely, pale shadow you can see right through."

Laura was startled by the girl's earnestness. With a bewildered smile she said, "You sound as if you might have seen her."

Anna's eyes met hers. "I'm not certain but that I have. There are few who live in Glengarry who do not feel they have seen her at one time or another. Least of all the Camerons."

"But why should she haunt the castle?"

Anna looked into the dying flames of the log fire. "It's not a pretty story," she replied, "but one that has been repeated down through the years. It all began when the castle was being built. One of the young workmen became infatuated with a village girl, Sheila MacLeod, but she wanted nothing to do with him. Maddened by her continual rejection of him, he tricked her into a secret rendezvous one moonlight night here on the castle grounds. As soon as she saw who was waiting for her, she tried to escape."

"And he killed her?"

"Yes. In a panic he decided to dispose of

the body so he couldn't be blamed for the murder. The upstairs section of the building was being completed and he carried Sheila's dead body up in his arms until he came to a section where a wall was being filled in. He placed her body behind the wall and carefully went to work bricking up the section. When the other workers arrived the next morning, they went on with the wall not knowing the guilty secret hidden by a certain area of it."

Laura asked, "Was the body discovered?"

"Not in time for the murderer to pay the penalty of his crime. It wasn't until about seventy years afterward, when Donald's father was having some changes made upstairs, that the wall was broken away and a skeleton discovered behind it. A skeleton with a locket that identified it as that of Sheila MacLeod. So now we all know why her spirit parades the corridors at night seeking an escape."

Laura shuddered. "It's a grisly story."

"And a true one," Anna assured her.

At that moment Donald returned to the room and came directly to them. "Mrs. Basset has dinner waiting for us," he said. With a smile for Laura, he added, "I know you must be hungry."

The dining room was about what Laura had expected. It was large with a high ceiling and dark wood-paneled walls. A still life hung here and there for decoration. The most striking feature of the room was the giant crystal chandelier which hung above the table and dominated it. Aunt Caroline sat hunched in a chair at the head of the table and Austin Cameron sat opposite her at the other end of it. Donald and Laura sat together at one side and Anna and Graham occupied the places across from them.

Laura was surprised to notice the resemblance between the farm manager and Donald except for the matter of complexion. Donald was dark in contrast to Graham's sandy hair. But their features were a lot alike. Mrs. Bassett made her appearance to serve the first course of steaming clam chowder. She was a buxom woman of middle-age with a good-natured, ruddy face and gray hair drawn back tight and coiled at the nape of her neck. When she served Laura, Donald introduced them.

"Welcome to the house, Mrs. Cameron," she said, a work-worn hand resting on her white apron. "We've all been anxious to see you arrive."

Laura thanked her and made a mental note that Mrs. Basset could be counted as one of the plus items in the picture of things confronting her. She tried to join in with the conversation conducted by the others at the table, but much of the time she was unable to follow what they were talking about. The local names and problems left her at a loss and she knew it would be some time before she became familiar enough with the Glengarry scene to take her part intelligently in such discussions.

Donald was extremely considerate of her at the table and insisted she eat all of the excellent fish filet Mrs. Basset had generously served her. He was the loving, solicitous husband in every way and she began to regret ever having doubted him. She was also keenly aware of the envious glances Anna flashed across the table at her when she thought she wasn't looking. Laura had a shrewd idea the lovely Anna was in love with Donald and probably had wanted to marry him herself. That could explain why Donald had mentioned her so little since he was probably aware of Anna's crush on him and embarrassed by it. It also explained the barely concealed hostility that Anna had shown towards her.

When dinner ended they all went back to the living room for coffee. Mrs. Basset brought in a huge silver tray with coffee pot and everything else on it, and then stayed to help Aunt Caroline pour. Graham took Donald aside to discuss some farm problem with him, and Laura found herself alone with Austin Cameron at the other side of the big room.

The stout, balding man stirred his coffee nervously. "I hope you'll be happy here," he said. "We're a tightly knit family group and it may take a while to understand us."

"I'm certain it won't take long," Laura replied, smiling, and took a sip of her own coffee. Then by way of making conversation she said, "Have you noticed what a resemblance there is between Graham and my husband?"

Austin chuckled. "Well, of course. And I'm interested in the fact you caught on so quickly."

She stared. "Caught on?"

"Yes." He leaned forward to her confidentially. "This is something not to be mentioned. Not even to Donald if you're wise. But Graham is a Glengarry man. The story goes that back half a century ago our grandfather had an illegitimate son by the

40

wife of a Graham."

"You mean?"

He looked wise. "No one can say for sure. But down through the years there has been a Graham strain that has looked a lot like the Camerons. And maybe that's why Donald and John Graham have identical features. And why Graham has as much love for the estate as my nephew does."

"I see," she said quietly.

"Naturally in a place as small as this the only way it's possible to live with such matters is to avoid mention of them altogether," Donald's uncle went on in his smooth way.

"Naturally," Laura agreed for want of something better to say. She was a trifle shocked by his revelation and wondered whether it might have been better if he'd not confided in her at all.

He gave her a sly wink. "But I thought it best you know in case you should repeat what you said to me just now to someone else in Glengarry. The wrong party could make quite a scandalous joke of it. If you understand me?"

"Of course," she assented, realizing he was right. A spiteful person could make a juicy morsel of gossip out of her innocent remark. Yet there was something in Austin

Cameron's manner of telling her the facts that made her dislike him intensely, even though that attitude mightn't be fair on her part.

"You and Anna should be grand company for one another," he went on.

"I look forward to that."

Austin Cameron smiled. "She is devoted to Donald. She has spent most of her life here. Her mother married me when Anna was little more than a baby, so she was brought up like one of the family. I'm sure she feels like a sister to Donald."

"How nice for them both," Laura said politely, and at the same time sensing that Austin Cameron, stout, balding and with the too-innocent face, was getting around to something.

"Devoted!" he repeated. "Even though there is no blood link between them." He paused, his eyes meeting hers. "Until Donald announced his marriage to you it had been my idea that one day he and Anna might become man and wife. But of course that is to be forgotten now. I'm sure Anna is as happy as we all are in his choice of you as a wife. After all, you bring so much to your marriage."

It was another one of those ambiguous remarks to upset her. Austin Cameron was plainly saying that she had brought Donald money whereas Anna had nothing to offer in that respect. It was just a different way of saying Donald had married her for her money.

She parried his remark by saying, "It was his music that brought us together."

"Of course!" He nodded. "I take it you are also a composer or perhaps play some instrument?"

"Neither. I'm just a simple patron of music. I served on a promotion committee for the Boston Symphony. We raised funds for it in various ways. So much money is required for ventures of this sort."

"True," he agreed. "And it was the Boston Symphony that played Donald's composition. We were all quite thrilled about it here. I tell you it has a Gaelic substance. I'm hoping to have the Halifax Symphony come to the college for a concert. If they do, I'll ask that they play Donald's work."

Laura was relieved to have the conversation take a different course. She commented, "Yes, that would be nice." At the same time she saw Graham leaving the living room and with her eyes she signaled Donald to come over and rescue her from Austin Cameron.

He did so, taking her arm and smiling for Austin's benefit. "Will you think me selfish if I steal my wife away for a few minutes alone with me?"

Austin Cameron chuckled. "I'd consider you a fool if you didn't do just that!"

As they left the room together she was aware of Anna's eyes following them. Anna had been seated talking with Aunt Caroline but it seemed she had not been giving the old woman her full attention. There was no doubt that she was finding it difficult to reconcile herself to the fact that Donald had a wife.

When they were alone in the reception hall Donald took her in his arms and kissed her ardently. Looking down at her with a smile, he asked, "Well, what do you make of them all?"

She hesitated, not wanting to hurt his feelings by telling him frankly that she found them all a bit difficult, and was sure her presence was resented. Instead she settled for, "It will take a while to really know them."

"But you have been able to talk with them?"

"Of course," she assured him, and without thinking went on to add, "We've discussed spooks and family skeletons and all kinds of things."

Donald's manner changed at once. He frowned. "What did you discuss?"

She saw the rapid fading of his good humor and was on her guard at once. With a forced smile she said quickly, "I mean I've heard about the castle's ghost. Anna told me the story of Sheila MacLeod."

"Scottish superstition!" he snapped. "I hope you don't listen to such wild talk. I can't understand why Anna would bring the subject up."

"It wasn't her fault, really. Your Aunt Caroline mentioned her first. And then I questioned Anna, who told me the story. It is a true tale, isn't it?"

"I suppose so," he said grudgingly. "It all took place a century ago. I like to think of the more pleasant aspects of this place. The parties it has seen, the great evenings of wedding celebrations and anniversaries. I tell you there were some grand occasions here in the old days."

She gave him a pert smile. "And are you forgetting this afternoon? Surely you and Graham gave me a true Scottish welcome."

A trace of good humor showed again. "I'm glad it meant something to you," he said. "There are still a few people you have to meet. My brother Frank, his wife, June, and my friends, Glenna and David Mac-Gregor."

"You mentioned them," she recalled. "Isn't he the town clerk?"

Donald nodded. "They're a fine couple. But they wouldn't think of intruding on your first night here. Of course my brother would have been here for dinner with June if she hadn't come down with another spell. She hasn't long to live, or so the doctors say."

"How awful for them!"

"Yes," he agreed with a sigh. "Frank needs her badly. He's a lonesome man without too many close friends. He devotes most of his time to his law practice and is regarded as the best lawyer in the district."

"Then he must do very well."

"As well as one would expect in a relatively poor rural area such as this," he said. "We are rich in tradition but poverty-stricken in nearly everything else."

"I'm sure Graham must be a very good manager for the estate," she said. "He strikes me as having a lot of intelligence."

Donald nodded slowly. "I count myself lucky he stays on. Though I can't say he will for long, the way things have been going. John Graham could command a larger salary almost anywhere he went."

46

"But he has affection for the estate and prefers to remain?"

"He thinks as much of it as I do," her husband said with a sigh.

Their conversation was broken by the front door bell ringing. Donald answered it, opening the door to reveal a young man of about his own size and age in a brown suede cap and car coat to match.

"Frank!" he said heartily and she knew this was his younger brother.

"Wanted to pay my respects," Frank Cameron said in a voice much like her husband's.

She stood anticipating his entrance with a smile, but when he came inside and removed his cap, she had a difficult time restraining a gasp of surprise and a still more awkward moment striving to retain her smile. She felt it must look frozen on her face.

Donald was saying, "This is Laura. My brother, Frank."

Frank was close to her now. He took her hand in his. "You're very lovely, Laura. I'm delighted for Donald's sake," he told her with warm sincerity.

"And you're fully as nice as I expected," she responded, struggling to sound natural. For no one had prepared her for the shock of Frank Cameron's appearance.

"Since I missed the ceremony, mind if I kiss the bride?" Frank Cameron genially asked his brother.

Donald shrugged. "I may mind but there is nothing I can do to stop you."

"I believe it's my legal right," Frank joked and leaned close to plant a chaste kiss on Laura's cheek. "Welcome to the bosom of our family, my dear."

She laughed. "I've been getting the red carpet treatment. I was given a welcome by a kilted piper."

"Playing the 'Cameron Airs' as composed by myself for bagpipes," her husband said, placing his arm around her.

Laura was grateful for this small gesture. She badly needed assurance. She tried not to stare at Donald's brother and found it awkward, for he was literally hairless!

Donald might have warned her. But perhaps he was so used to it, or even sensitive of his brother's condition. Not only was Frank's head completely bereft of hair, he had no eyebrows, nor eyelashes, not even a hint of beard or skin hair of any kind. It gave him an odd, egg-like appearance. She felt he might resemble Donald some in features, though it was impossible to tell in the face of his affliction. He looked much older than his years.

Gradually she managed to adjust herself to the great, white, oval face and head. She said, "I'm looking forward to meeting June."

Frank Cameron at once looked forlorn. "She's not well tonight. Not well at all. She sends her regrets. And she asked that you come to visit us as soon as you can."

"I'll do that," Laura promised.

"June is a brilliant woman," Frank added, "even though she is my wife. She was a private secretary in one of the most prominent law firms in Halifax before she married me. I'm sure she would have found something to occupy her talents here if her health hadn't failed."

Donald continued to keep his comforting arm lightly around her as if he sensed she had been upset by his brother's strange appearance. He explained, "Frank's cottage is part of the estate. It's not far away even if you don't use the shortcut."

"I don't advise her using that until she's more familiar with the country," Frank commented with a smile. "It's a back road that cuts off a half mile to the cottage. But it's a shelf of a road that runs on the rim of a deep chasm. Dangerous unless you know it well. When June was driving I never allowed her to use it."

"Probably best to avoid walking there as well," her husband agreed. "It's lonely and the main road only takes about ten minutes longer." He glanced toward the living room. "Perhaps we should go back with the others. I know Aunt Caroline will want to talk with you, Frank."

They moved on back into the living room. Laura now found herself much in the company of the veteran Aunt Caroline and Frank, who it seemed was her favorite. Frank had a fine personality and knew exactly how to draw the old woman out. In no time he had her talking about days she had known back in Scotland. It seemed she had married and gone back there to live until sometime in the dim past when her husband had died and she'd returned to spend her declining years at the family estate.

Her wrinkled face took on a smile as she stared into the blazing log fire. "The New Year is the true time for Scots to celebrate," she reminisced for them. "I remember many a New Year in Edinburgh. My husband would drive me downtown on our way to a grand party. We would see crowds gathered at the Tron to wait the New Year in."

Frank interrupted to explain to Laura, "The Tron Church is at High Street and the Bridges in Edinburgh. It has four clocks, one on each side of the steeple, and was built in 1647. On the night of Hogmanay, the 31st of December, it's the place where thousands gather on the street outside to welcome the New Year."

"Aye!" The old woman shifted in her chair and chuckled. "I can see them even now gathered on the pavements. The shops and banks with their windows boarded and the drink flowing like the River Clyde! By eleven the crowd is big enough to stop all traffic. And as the minutes pass the frenzy grows. Then the singing, the mouth organs, the dancing, all stop as eyes fasten on the Tron clocks. The magic minute comes close. Then the minute hands touch midnight and a bell tolls. There is a gasp, a shout, a roar. Hats, bottles and shoes fly in the air! People are kissing, clutching, dancing, and alive!" She paused to nod reflectively. "Aye! Alive! That's the main thing! And who of us will be here next year to celebrate another Hogmanay?"

"You will, Aunt Caroline, and that's for certain," Frank Cameron said in his warm way. "You are an inspiration to all of us!"

But the old woman had faded off into some corner of the past again. "Your father will be upset," she murmured. "He won't approve at all. There are dark days at hand for this house."

Frank moved Laura gently away and whispered. "Let her be. It seems to work best if she's let alone to come out of these spells."

"It's too bad," she said. "Otherwise she's such a wonderful person."

They joined Donald and the others. Shortly afterward Anne Caroline raised herself out of the chair. Leaning heavily on her cane, she made her way out of the living room. She disdained any help from them but paused to kiss Frank goodnight on her way out. Donald assured Laura there was no need to worry, Mrs. Basset kept an eye on the stairs and would join the old woman on the first landing and see her safely to bed.

Frank was the next to go, pleading concern about his wife alone at home as his reason. Laura realized that she was desperately tired, and making her goodnights to Austin and his stepdaughter, Anna, she left with Donald. Again she was conscious of Anna's eyes fixed on them with jealousy.

But once she and Donald reached the

privacy of their room she forgot the envious eyes and was satisfied with the mere happiness of being with the man she loved. There were problems to be solved, she knew that well enough, but as long as she and this handsome man who had given her his name continued to be in love she felt they could all be cleared up.

She was in bed, her head on the pillow and her eyes closed, when Donald came to sit on the edge of the bed beside her. He spoke in a gentle tone, "I'm sorry I didn't mention about Frank. I know it bothered you."

Laura opened her eyes to stare up at him. She gave a small smile. "It was a surprise."

He frowned. "He was born that way. Dreadful for him. But once people know him they seem to forget his appearance."

"I know. He's very nice."

"I wish I had his disposition," Donald admitted. "And when you think of his years of trouble with a sick wife you must admit he has a special kind of grace to carry on as he has."

"I hope I didn't make it too obvious that he startled me," she said.

Her husband smiled sadly. "You did very well. I felt I was to blame for the situation.

I guess I didn't mention it because it's something we never discuss here. The family records tell of a cousin two generations back who suffered from the same lack of hair. Apparently it's a Cameron blight!"

"It isn't all that important," she told him. "Your brother is a fine man."

"And you're an understanding wife," Donald told her quietly as he bent down to kiss her goodnight.

She fell asleep almost at once. But it was a sleep troubled by weird dreams in which the events of the day became changed in a fantastic manner. The faces and voices of the members of the family whom she'd so recently met crowded her nightmare in a mocking parade. Anna and she had a violent argument, ending in a struggle between them. Laura cried out her anger and resentment of Anna's behavior.

She came fully awake with a scream on her lips. It took her a moment to realize where she was as she sat up in bed staring into the darkness of the room. Then she turned to waken Donald and found he was not at her side. Her hand reached out to feel the sheet which was still warm from his body. But he was not there. This discovery startled her and she could not imagine why he had left her, or where he might have gone.

"Donald!" she called out, thinking he might be in the room. But there was no answer from the shadows.

She waited, not knowing what to do. Then she heard a soft sound, a kind of moaning, whimpering sound. With growing fear she knew that it had come from the hallway. At the same time she realized the bedroom door was partly ajar and any noise from outside would easily reach her. Donald must have left the door that way when he went out.

Scarcely daring to breathe, she waited, her eyes fixed in the direction of the door. Then she heard the whimpering again and she saw it. The figure in flowing white came into full view as very slowly it glided past the open door. A ghostly female, with long silvery hair, just as Anna had described. A veil-like covering hid her face and in her hand she carried a flickering, white candle.

In a moment she had vanished, leaving Laura chilled with terror. She could not believe what she had just seen. She refused to believe it. This fantastic story of Sheila MacLeod's ghost must have preyed on her mind and brought on this macabre vision. She must fight against the terror of it.

Not fully aware of her purpose, she slipped out of bed and put on slippers and dressing gown. She hesitated in the darkness for a moment and then, anxious to find Donald, slowly made her way to the open doorway. Again she paused, knowing that she was trembling and nauseated with fear, before she went out into the hallway. There was still no sound, nor any sign of Donald. She turned and slowly made her way along the hall in the same direction in which she thought the creature in white had vanished.

She forced herself to edge ahead, one faltering step after another, and all the time hoping that Donald might suddenly put in an appearance. She was bewildered and fearful at his desertion of her in this way. But there was nothing to break the soft, after-midnight silence of the old castle. There was no movement in the shadows to announce another presence. She groped her way on in the almost pitch darkness.

Then, at a distance ahead, she thought she saw a dim shaft of flickering light. It made her halt with a gasp but after a moment her curiosity drove her on. She went forward until she came to an open door through which the ghostly flame from a candle broke the gloom. She halted at the door and stared into the room with frightened eyes. She saw the candle on what appeared to be a high table.

Swallowing hard to help contain her terror, she took a halting step into the room. She scanned the surrounding darkness for some hint of the white figure whose candle rested on the plain table ahead. The room seemed to be empty. Again she stepped closer to the candle, and closer!

Then with a small cry of fear, her hand raised to her mouth, she halted. For the thing she had taken for a table was not a table but a plain, oak coffin on a stand. The candle flickered alarmingly as she stood there transfixed with horror and let her eyes creep toward the open upper section of the coffin. It was quite empty! At the same instant that she made this discovery she was chilled to the marrow by the sound of footsteps behind her!

CHAPTER THREE

The sudden movement in the near darkness behind her, together with the eerie sight of the candle set on the coffin, caused her to go rigid with terror. She stood there, horror-stricken, her eyes fixed on the faltering flame of the candle, expecting some ghostly breath to snuff it out even as she watched and waited for the skeleton hands of the long-dead to seize her.

When she felt herself gripped firmly by the unseen presence behind, she weakly closed her eyes and murmured a feeble word of protest. Near fainting, she was wheeled around.

"What in Heaven's name are you doing in here?" It was Donald's familiar voice that posed the anxious question.

Not completely believing it could be Donald, she allowed her eyes to open reluctantly to stare up into his serious face. He was wearing a dressing gown over his pajamas and seemed nearly as startled as she was.

"You terrified me!" she whispered.

"And you gave me a start. What possessed you to start wandering about in the middle of the night?"

"I awakened from a nightmare and found you'd left the room."

He looked embarrassed. "I'm sorry," he said. "I wasn't able to sleep, so I went down to the study. There were some estate papers I wanted to look at."

She gave a great sigh as the worst of her fear left her. She explained, "I was upset. I couldn't imagine what was wrong." She paused. "You left the door partly open."

"I don't remember," he said awkwardly. "I may have. I've been used to sleeping there alone."

There was still a hint of terror in her eyes as she recalled the eerie figure. "A woman in white passed in the hallway carrying a candle. I called out but there was no answer!"

"A figure in white!" His tone was incredulous.

She gazed up at him soberly. "Yes. A ghostly figure. I could only think of that murdered girl, Sheila MacLeod!"

Donald looked angry. "Of course they had to scare you with that story," he said. "You probably had a nightmare. Thought you saw someone in the hall."

Laura turned slowly and indicated the candle on the coffin. "What about the candle?"

He hesitated and then the perplexity on his face gave way to relief. "I can give you the answer to both the candle and your ghostly figure."

She stared at him. "Yes?"

"It was Aunt Caroline you saw."

"Aunt Caroline!"

He nodded. "Without a question. You know her mental state. We haven't been able to stop her wandering about at night. In her nightgown and with her white hair tumbling about her shoulders she could easily suggest a silver-haired ghost. Especially in the quick glimpse you had of her by feeble candlelight."

"It could have been her," Laura said, forced to agree.

"There is no doubt about it," her husband said firmly. "You were only half awake and ready to see her as a ghost. The candle here on the coffin in this way proves my theory to be correct."

Laura said, "Why do you say that?"

"This coffin is Aunt Caroline's," he said with a sigh. "Don't bother asking me why she insists on keeping it here. It dates back to the old days when coffins were hard to come by in the winter season. There were no good roads or cars and when a village didn't have an undertaker it was fairly common for older people to carefully select their coffins and keep them on hand. Aunt Caroline has had this one waiting here in this room for more than five years."

She gave the empty oak coffin with its ornate white satin lining a furtive glance again. "How grotesque!" she exclaimed.

"Aunt Caroline is impossible to reason with," Donald said. "We've found it easier to go along with her eccentric ideas. I'm sorry you had to suffer tonight because of them."

Gradually she was coming to the point where his explanations seemed convincing enough. She recognized that the gloomy atmosphere of the old castle and her own fears had combined to make her open to easy suggestion that she'd witnessed a ghostly visitor. Certainly his theory that she had seen the old woman wandering in the hallway was borne out by the discovery of the candle on top of the coffin.

She gave a small shiver, as much a pro-test of her mind as of her body, although the midnight cold of the old house was insinuating its clammy presence and caus-

ing her discomfort. She was also ashamed
for having caused a scene and for having
worried about Donald not being at her
side when she awakened. But it underlined
the fact that he was still seriously concerned about something, and made her
decide all over again that in the morning
she would insist on his frankly telling her
what was wrong.

He moved toward the coffin and, leaning
over, blew out the candle. They were
engulfed in shadows again, but he quickly
put a protective arm around her, led her
out into the hallway and back toward their
room.

When she was safely in bed, he said,
"You mustn't allow yourself to be awed by
this house. It is not the unhappy place you
seem to imagine it. Cameron Castle once
knew a warm family life. It is my hope that
it may do so again."

"I'm sorry to have been so foolish," she
apologized, staring up at him with fond
eyes. "It began when I found you gone.
Don't ever leave me!"

He laughed quietly. "Let that be the
least of your fears!" He kissed her goodnight once again.

Secure in the knowledge that he was
beside her once more, she succumbed to

the warmth of the bed and sank into a deep sleep. She awoke in the morning feeling much refreshed with the midnight episode hardly lingering in her memory. Donald had already dressed and gone downstairs for his breakfast. She was about to get up and follow him when there was a knock on the door and Mrs. Basset let herself in. She was carrying a breakfast tray and wore a broad smile on her face.

"Now don't you move your pretty self from the bed," she admonished, as she bustled forward and set the tray on the bedside table. She went over and drew the crimson drapes on first one window and then the other, allowing the bright morning sunshine to flood in.

Turning to Laura she announced, "It's a truly lovely day. Much more fitting for your welcome than yesterday's dark clouds." She came back to the tray and removed the white napkin that covered it. "I hope you like oatmeal, ma'am."

"Very much," Laura smiled.

"Then that's good." Mrs. Basset sounded pleased. "It's a staple here. We Scots have our favorite dishes. Oatmeal is surely one of them." She went on arranging the tray. "And do you know in the north of Scotland the way of eating porridge is to serve the milk in a separate dish and then dip a spoon full of porridge in the milk." She finished with a laugh and placed the tray on the bed before Laura.

Laura protested, "I'm not used to such waiting on. In the future I'll come down for breakfast."

Mrs. Basset smiled. "As you like. It makes no difference. I always bring the old one up her breakfast, in any case. It means little bother to prepare an extra tray."

"There's no need," Laura assured her as she picked up her glass of orange juice. "I know you are short of help and every extra step must count."

The housekeeper sighed. "It is a big place, ma'am. And dear knows what you'll think of the condition of it. I've had to let some of the rooms go."

"I can understand that."

"I try to keep this main wing neat and tidy and that is about the best I can manage along with looking after the kitchen."

Laura nodded as she continued with her breakfast. "I will try and help you. At least I can look after this room."

Mrs. Basset looked startled. "No need of that. None of the others do."

She lifted her eyebrows. "I'd think Miss

Gordon could take care of her own room and that of her stepfather."

"Miss Anna isn't that sort, ma'am," the housekeeper said simply. "She expects everything to be done when she comes back from the school."

"Really?" Laura was surprised. "I must talk to her about it sometime."

"I wouldn't if I were you, ma'am," the housekeeper answered quickly. Then as if realizing that her unasked for advice might cause Laura to wonder, she added, "I think she might specially resent it. I mean, coming from you."

Laura looked up from the tray and once again decided that the housekeeper was a woman of sound judgment on whom she could depend. "Thank you, Mrs. Basset," she said. "I hadn't thought of that side of it. I expect you're right."

The housekeeper left her to continue her breakfast alone and she considered what they had just discussed. Mrs. Basset was plainly aware that Anna resented her coming to Cameron Castle as its new mistress. This meant the girl was bound to be especially touchy of any criticism coming from her. Laura knew that Anna would continue to hate her for having won Donald's love. It was a difficult situation and she would have to proceed with any suggestions in an extremely tactful way.

When she finished breakfast she quickly took a shower and dressed. She was on her way downstairs by nine thirty. The great house seemed strangely quiet, except for the loud ticking of a grandfather's clock that stood in the reception hall near the entrance to the living room. Laura paused to study it a moment and could tell it was of ancient vintage, as were most of the furnishings in the old house.

She knew that the study was in the rear of the house, and so made her way along the dark corridor that led to that part of the mansion. She hoped that Donald would still be at home, and she would be able to take up the problem that had been disturbing her. As she reached the far end of the hall she found a door on the right partly opened. Through the doorway she saw Donald seated at his desk, poring over a long, legal-looking document with a frown on his face.

Hesitating a moment, she knocked softly on the study door. At once he answered, lifting his head and calling, "Yes?"

She pushed the door fully open. "I want to talk with you," she said, entering.

"Of course," he was polite in tone as he

rose from his chair and came forward to pull up a chair for her opposite his desk. "I wondered when you might be down."

Laura smiled at him as she settled in the chair primly. "Mrs. Basset brought me my breakfast and that saved time."

"Good," he said as he closed the door leading to the hallway and took the chair behind his desk again. "You must get her to show you around. I would do it now but I have to go to Sydney to look after some estate business."

His news suddenly depressed her. "Will you be gone long?"

He shook his head. "No. I should be back shortly after dinner. You'll have plenty to keep you occupied while I'm away."

"Of course," she agreed, still unhappy with the news but not wanting to let him know how she felt. It seemed he was leaving her too soon. She needed his support on this first full day as the new mistress of the rambling stone mansion. Her eyes wandered to the study walls with their shelves of books. There was a fireplace in this room as well, since the building dated beyond the advent of central heating by many years. The single casement window looked out over the lawn toward the distant range of mountains.

Donald's sensitive face showed a faint smile. "Make Anna give you some facts about the place when she returns from school. But don't let her stuff you with any more ghost stories. We've had enough trouble on that score."

Laura felt her cheeks redden. She said, "Don't worry about me. I'll manage nicely. I came here to talk to you before you leave."

"I haven't much time. What is it you want to say?"

She decided to come directly to the point. "I know you've been upset ever since you received that wire in Boston. I feel certain it has something to do with the financial problems of the estate, and I want you to honestly tell me how things stand."

He stared at her and she was afraid he was going to spoil everything by making a complete denial of any money problems. But as he looked at her his manner changed and he finally settled back in his chair with a deep sigh.

"I guess there is no point in making up a story," he sighed. "It seems that already you are able to read my mind."

"A wife's perogative," she told him.

He wrinkled his high forehead. "I guess I

owe you the facts. Maybe I'm even late in offering them to you. But I hoped it would be something I'd not have to mention. I didn't expect a crisis so soon."

"What sort of crisis?"

Donald stared at her unhappily. "In spite of Graham's efforts the farm has not earned enough to pay our bills here. We've been going steadily into debt. I've devoted too much time to my music and that has complicated things."

"But your music is important!"

He waved this aside. "Not as important as the estate. It may be years until I am able to make any name as a composer. I could wind up never earning real money from my music. And in the meantime I could lose the castle." He said this in tragic desperation as if it was the worst thing he could imagine happening.

"I'm sure you will be recognized as a leading composer one day," she insisted. "I want you to go on with it."

He shook his head. "I don't see how it will be possible." With his eyes meeting hers directly, he added, "It looks as if I shouldn't even have gotten married. I doubt that I can afford a wife."

"Donald!" she said reprovingly.

He got up quickly and came over to put

a hand on her shoulder. "What I mean is, it isn't fair to you. I can't offer you a proper home here with the place run-down as it is. And there are all the other things I'd like to be able to give you and can't."

"You love me and that's the most important thing," she assured him with a smile, as she reached up to cover his hand with her own. "It's all that I ask."

He sighed. "I know you were worried about the telegram I received in Boston and my reaction to it. I guess I'll have to tell you the truth about it."

"Please," she urged.

"It was from the bank in Sydney which has the mortgage on this place. They informed me that unless I could raise some cash at once they'd have to offer the castle to the highest bidder. You can understand why I've been upset ever since."

"You should have told me right away," she said.

"And completely spoil our wedding day?"

Laura decided quickly. "How much cash do you need?"

He shrugged and named a sum high in the thousands. Then he said, "I'm going to see the bank manager in Sydney today and ask for more time. Beg for it if necessary. If he refuses I don't know what I'll do."

"You needn't beg for money," she told him quietly.

He seemed surprised. "What do you mean?"

"I'll write you a check for what you need," she told him in an even voice. "You can take it with you today and settle the whole affair."

"But you can't do that," he protested. "Put your money in this house!"

"I consider it a good investment," she assured him. "And I want you to be free of this worry so you can enjoy working at your music. And so we can have some happiness in our marriage."

Donald's face brightened and he studied her with a baffled surprise. "I can hardly believe you mean it. I don't dare believe it!"

"But I do," she said, rising.

He broke into a delighted smile. "But this will solve everything," he exclaimed. "Once we get the old debt paid off I know Graham can keep our present expenses in line with the income from the farm."

"I'll get my checkbook," she promised. "It's upstairs in the room."

She found the checkbook, brought it to the study, and wrote out a check to cover the exact amount he'd mentioned. He took it like a small boy receiving a prize, and he was ecstatic in his praise of her and in his declarations of undying affection. It was a happy moment and not until he left to drive to Sydney did she feel a strange reversal of emotions.

Back in her room, she was ready to return the checkbook into her dresser drawer when suddenly it came to her that everything Aunt Alice had warned her about was turning out exactly as she'd predicted. The happiness and confidence she'd so recently known were replaced by doubts and consternation. Laura frowned at the checkbook and swiftly put it in the drawer and closed it. Once again money had failed to bring her any lasting happiness.

Aunt Alice had insisted she was being married for her wealth. Then both Anna and her stepfather, Austin Cameron, had managed to convey the same impression. It seemed that everyone was of this opinion. Were they all secretly amused? It was a hateful thought but one she couldn't help facing now that she was alone.

She comforted herself with the knowledge that Donald hadn't wanted to take the money from her. She actually had to make the suggestion and insist that he let her pay the debt on the castle. Still, he had taken the check without too much objection in the end. Had his moods all been carefully presented to produce this result? Had he deliberately baited her while pretending not to want any aid from her? She knew it was possible and she didn't want to believe it.

To believe it would mean too many things, including the end of their love. The marriage would be a failure and a travesty within this short period of days. Her estimation of Donald as a man would have been proven woefully wrong. And since she didn't want to accept any of these answers she must hold on to her conviction that his marrying her had nothing to do with his financial plight.

It was true she had known him only a short time. That had been one of her Aunt's chief arguments against the match. But she had found him to be a sensitive, thoughtful person, incapable of cruelty or meanness of any sort. And she couldn't believe that he had been able to deceive her with a concealed side to his character.

It was an unfortunate coincidence that this money trouble had come to a head at the same time as their marriage, but she couldn't blame that on Donald, or hold it against him. Knowing of his love for the estate, she had done the right thing in underwriting his debt and in giving him a chance to retain it. The best thing she could do now was to put the whole matter out of her mind and concentrate on finding the happiness she hoped for in her marriage.

With this positive thought she faced the day. She went down to see Mrs. Basset, who gave her a short tour of the main wing, being careful, Laura noted, to let her see only the rooms in good order.

"You don't want to see the empty rooms with their dampness and broken plaster," she announced. "There are plenty of them, filled with cobwebs and spiders, but they're never used and why should I depress you by taking you the rounds of them."

Laura smiled. "I'll get Donald to do that later."

"The poor man will only worry more when he sees the decay that is going on in the east and west wings again," Mrs. Basset warned her. "I can't even manage to keep the windows in those rooms clean. It's a grimy view of the outside you get from them."

"What about the cellar?" Laura asked. "Is it in use?"

"Not all of it," the housekeeper replied, with a sad shaking of her gray head. "More than two-thirds of it is locked off and in a dreadful state. But that seems to be the way of things these days. If we only had more help."

They went down the same corridor that Laura had visited the previous night and when the housekeeper opened the door of the room with the coffin lying in state in it, she confided to her, "Belongs to the old woman. Or maybe I should say it the other way around. No matter! It's a pesky business! I don't approve at all. It fair gives me the creeps knowing it's up here, empty and waiting!"

Laura managed a faint smile. "I know what you mean," she said.

"Don't let her worry you," Mrs. Basset advised her. "She likes to rule the roost. And I don't think she's a bit more pleased about Mr. Donald marrying you than some of the other ladies in the house. Begging your pardon, ma'am!"

She knew what the housekeeper meant. That Aunt Caroline might be as resentful of her coming to the castle as Anna was. Yet, when she talked with Aunt Caroline on the sun porch after lunch, she seemed friendly enough.

Aunt Caroline had a favorite chair in every room. In the glassed-in sun porch she had a large, heavy rocker positioned so that she could see the front lawn and the winding road below. She had the usual shawl around her shoulders, this one of blue, silky material, and her hair was carefully done in the same upsweep as the day before. Laura had an idea that Mrs. Basset must assist the old woman with her hair as well as doing all her other work. It was no wonder the cleaning of the great mansion continually kept getting ahead of her.

Aunt Caroline regarded her with an appraising smile. "You look pale today, girl," she said, resting her hands on the head of the silver cane. "Why don't you go out for a walk? You haven't seen much of the place and the air will do you good."

"I may," Laura agreed. "I don't imagine Donald will be home until late and I doubt that Anna will care to take a stroll when she comes home from teaching school."

"Don't count on that one," Aunt Caroline sniffed with distaste. "She's just like her mother! Full of airs! I don't know why Austin ever brought the woman into the family. But then I daresay he cares more for his Gaelic than he has for any female! The blood runs thin in Austin!"

"He tells me they have a great festival at the college every summer," Laura said, anxious to change the subject since she was somewhat embarrassed at the old woman's frank summing up of Austin and his stepdaughter. "I understand you have Highland games on the estate as well."

"We do," Aunt Caroline said, showing much interest. "We're the last of the big estates to have them. The rest are just town and county fairs. But the Camerons have held a meet right down through the years. It's a grand affair with Highland dancing, tugs-of-war, high-jumping, shot-putting, and pipe bands you can hear for miles, along with the tossing of the caber!"

This last was new to Laura and she raised questioning eyebrows. "Tossing the caber?"

The old woman in the chair chuckled and then coughed. When she had finally subdued the hacking coughing fit she looked up at Laura with her bright, old eyes gleaming with amusement. "You'll not have heard of the caber," she remarked. "Well, that's not strange. It's a Scots game. You'll see it played come June when the strongest of the young men toss great logs like telephone poles end over end. It is a man's game. My own husband was a champion!"

Laura smiled. "I'm making new discoveries here all the time."

But Aunt Caroline was no longer listening to her, the old woman's blue eyes had lost some of their brightness and she was now staring down at the paved highway that wound far below.

"I've watched yon road when the ox teams plied its red dirt," she said in a vague tone. "And now they speed along it like the wind, and I'm still waiting. Still waiting for him to come. It's not right for a husband to desert his wife. Not right!"

Laura had the weird feeling of a veil suddenly descending between her and the aged woman in the rocking chair. She looked at the thin, parchment-colored face, the distant look in the blue eyes, the veined hands restlessly working on the cane's silver head, and it seemed that Aunt Caroline had drifted off into a different world. Certainly her wandering had begun again, since she questioned why her long dead husband had not returned. Feeling uncomfortable in the presence of this exhibition of age and decay, Laura carefully withdrew from the sun porch, leaving the old woman alone.

Deciding to take Aunt Caroline's advice, she went upstairs and put on her topcoat and kerchief. Even though the sun was shining, she knew the day was still cool enough. Spring came with reluctance to this northeastern section of Nova Scotia. She went out and across the front lawn to the flagpole, which was higher than she had suspected. From there she crossed the still somewhat colorless and winter-touched grass to the brink of the cliffs overlooking the main highway. The ground sloped down at a severe angle from where she stood and there were places where it was sheer lined rock, while now and again there were leveling off spots with ever-greens on them. Still, there was no really flat terrain until the highway and no doubt this had been artificially constructed over the years, for on the far side of it the ground again descended with occasional patches of evergreens and bushes until it reached the beach and the sea beyond.

She eyed the white-capped waves as they rolled into shore. It was a rugged place where both the land and ocean maintained a sullen struggle for supremacy. The rocky beach defying the greedy wash of the great waves, day in and day out. And now, as late afternoon arrived, the bright skies were clouding over again and it was becoming gray and cold once more.

With a slight hunching, Laura pressed her hands firmly in her pockets as she turned and strolled slowly back toward Cameron Castle. The great stone building seemed larger than when she had first glimpsed it yesterday. Alarmingly big and grim! She would have liked to have begun her marriage in some modest, modern home, but this place meant so much to Donald. She hoped that he was having a day of triumph in Sydney, paying off his debt to the banker.

She continued to walk around the end of the east wing which was obviously deserted from the vacant, grimy windows that stared darkly at her as she passed. They gave her the feeling that legions of ghostly eyes were watching her progress across the lawn and not approving. As she rounded the building she had a view of the several barns and smaller outbuildings. She was surprised to see Graham in earnest conversation with Anna Gordon in front of the largest barn. Anna was carrying some books under her arm and when she turned and saw Laura approaching, she seemed upset. She turned back and said something quickly to the tall, young farm manager and then hurried off towards the house in the opposite direction.

Coming up to John Graham, Laura ventured, "I seemed to have frightened her away."

Graham smiled. "Not really. She meant to go inside anyway. She stayed to tell me some happenings in the village."

"Oh!" She tried to sound casual. He might be reminding her in a polite way that she was still an outsider. Again she had the feeling that his eyes were fixed on her too closely; that there was a hardness in them she could not account for.

"Donald went to Sydney," she said. "I don't suppose he'll be back until late."

"It could be eight or nine o'clock," Graham said, his eyes never leaving her. "Well, I must get on with my work."

It was said almost in the manner of a brusque dismissal and she walked back to the house feeling depressed again. Had she any friends in the big house? She doubted it. They were all presenting a cold front of acceptance toward her, but it was no more than a front. Not one of them regarded her as other than an unwelcome intruder. Perhaps Aunt Caroline was the sole exception.

And she was a trifle mad! Laura smiled wryly to herself.

Dinner proved an ordeal. Anna did not appear, her stepfather saying that she had a headache. Graham, quiet as usual, arrived at the table late and left early. Aunt Caroline was vaguer than Laura had ever seen her and chattered with Austin Cameron incessantly about people who Laura was sure had long been in their graves, from the way he carried on his end of the conversation. After dinner they both vanished to their rooms, leaving Laura alone.

She read in the living room for a while, then became anxious for Donald's return. She thought he must be along soon and on an impulse decided to put on her coat and kerchief and go out on the lawn to wait for his headlights to show on the highway. She planned to be outside to greet him. It was cold, dark and lonely on the lawn and she had only been there a short while when she decided she should return to the cold comfort of the house. She was making her way across the lawn when she heard the footsteps close behind her. Alarmed, she began to run. Then something caught her throat.

CHAPTER FOUR

Laura was conscious of heavy breathing behind her, and then of something being slipped over her head and tightening around her neck. With a frightened, choked cry she lifted her hands to try and free the increasing pressure of the cord that was now biting into her flesh. As she vainly clawed to free herself from the torture, she was dimly aware of a light flashing on in one of the upstairs windows at the front of the mansion.

Even as she struggled, her heart gave a great leap and she was filled with hope that this might be someone coming to her rescue. Her attacker reacted to the sudden light by slackening the cord slightly, and she managed a hoarse scream. At the same time she turned a little and for just a fleeting second caught a glimpse of her maniacal assailant. For that brief instant she stared into the face of her husband. Then, with a quivering moan, she blacked out in total shock.

The grass was moist and she groaned as she turned a little. It had been so restful.

The velvet darkness had given her a surcease of thought and of any need to struggle further, and now this moment of deep peace was to be spoiled. She groaned in protest again as someone shook her with what seemed needless savagery.

"Mrs. Cameron, can you hear me? Answer me!"

Still dazed and protesting as much against this intrusion on her brief interlude of peace as against anything else she moaned weakly, "No! No!"

Again she was shaken, and this time lifted to an upright position, while the same voice questioned her with frantic urgency. "Mrs. Cameron, are you all right?"

Laura opened her eyes and gazed at the intruder blearily. As consciousness returned, she recalled the terrifying experience that had left her limp on the grass, and she gave a feeble scream.

"No hysterics, please, Mrs. Cameron," the man's voice begged.

Now she was able to remember everything clearly, although her head was still reeling. She stared through the darkness and was able to make out the dim outline of John Graham's rugged countenance. So he was the one who had saved her.

She said, "Did you see who it was?"

"No, I saw no one," he said. "I thought I heard a scream out here and came to find out. I discovered you on the grass unconscious."

"And there was no one else near?"

"No," he said. "What happened?"

"Somebody attacked me. Tried to kill me."

Graham, still holding her by the arms, hesitated a moment. Then he said, "You must be joking."

"It's no joke," she protested. "Something was slipped around my neck. A cord, I think. It must still be here."

He produced a flashlight from his pocket. Turning on the beam carefully, he scanned the ground in their vicinity. "I didn't take time to use this before," he said. After thoroughly searching the grass close to them, he announced, "No sign of a cord here. Did you get a look at whoever it was?"

Now came her turn to hesitate. She could not reveal the sickening truth at this moment. The face she had glimpsed for such a short period had looked remarkably like her husband's. It had seemed to be Donald in that horrifying second of revelation. Now, in retrospect, she thought that very likely this had been a wild mistake on her part. She had been expecting Donald, his face was imprinted on her mind, and when she had caught this frightening vision of a face in the feeble light from the window, it had borne a resemblance to Donald's and she had at once jumped to the conclusion it was him. But it couldn't have been! Donald hadn't returned from Sydney yet. And what reason could he have for doing such a thing? She couldn't accuse her own husband of trying to strangle her. She couldn't even allow herself to think it had been him.

She said, "I only had a glimpse of him for a moment. The face wasn't clear."

Graham had the flashlight pointed directly on her face so that its strong beam made her blink. He queried, "You can't remember anything about him?"

"It was a man," she replied. "I'm sure of that. And would you mind, please, not pointing the light directly in my eyes. My head is splitting."

"I'm sorry," he apologized. "I didn't think."

"It's all right," she murmured in weary resignation. "So there was no cord."

"No cord," he said, as if he doubted one had ever existed. He casually let the beam of the flashlight go over the surrounding area again. "You haven't any idea what he looked like?"

She knew he wasn't satisfied with her previous answer and suspected she was holding something back, but she couldn't bring herself to tell him who she had thought it was. It came to her wryly that she might as well say her attacker looked like him. John Graham did bear a remarkable resemblance to her husband. And this brought on a new train of thought. Could it have been Graham? Had he been scared off by the light and then returned to pretend he was her rescuer? It was possible. But again, not likely. She seemed to recall that her attacker wore a weird, battered hat and something dark, like an old topcoat, perhaps, closed tightly around his throat so that no shirt, tie or collar had been visible. She was picking these bits and pieces from her memory of the moment and she was not at all sure of any of them.

"I was too frightened to think coherently. To register any proper impressions. I expect that is why I blacked out. That and the pressure on my throat."

John Graham grunted. "You really haven't anything to offer in the way of a clue."

"I'm afraid not," she said abjectly. "Except it did happen and I was the victim."

He gave her a quick glance. "I didn't mean to sound unsympathetic," he told her in his dry way. "Are you feeling any better?"

"A good deal."

"Then let me help you inside."

Laura at once panicked. "Don't let us make a big fuss over this. I'd rather not mention it to the others until I'm able to explain it."

"That may never be."

"I'll take that chance," she told him. "Let's make our way into the house without attracting any attention."

"Not likely you have anything to worry about. I think they've all gone to bed. At least they are all upstairs. We may as well go in the front door."

She allowed him to take her by the arm and guide her across the lawn to the main entrance of the great stone house. She saw that the light which had been turned on briefly at the moment of her attack was now out. The window was again dark. She made a mental note to find out whose room it was. In retrospect it struck her that there could be another interpretation to the light that so suddenly came on at that vital moment. It could have been the signal of a collaborator in the attack against her, a signal from someone in the house to warn whoever it was had tried to throttle her.

She waited weakly as John Graham opened the door, and when they were in the dimly lighted reception hall, she stood with small girl dependence as he helped her off with her coat and then solemnly assisted in untying her rumpled kerchief.

"Let me look at your throat," he said, and proceeded to make a minute inspection of it. She stood feeling embarrassed as he held back the strands of her blonde hair to check carefully. He sighed when he had finished. Then he asked, "You're certain you don't want me to call down Austin Cameron or Anna?"

"Quite certain."

"Anna would be glad to be of help."

She felt a slight anger at his insistence. "I've already told you I don't want either of them to know."

His rugged face showed perplexity. "You're a lady with definite ideas," he said.

"I'm a lady with weak knees at this moment," she said. "I feel I might faint again if I don't find a chair, and soon!"

Graham grasped her quickly around the waist. "I think I should call the village doctor."

"No," she said with a sigh. "Just find me a chair."

"Come in here," he suggested. "A glass or two of wine should help right now." He helped her into the living room and into the nearest easy chair. He snapped on a handy table lamp and then hurried down the long, shadowed room to the sideboard.

She felt better as soon as she sat down. Though she was still nauseated and a little dizzy, she was able to think with relative clarity, and she found her position preposterous. She probably should have taken his advice and roused the whole household. But to what benefit? Probably Anna and her stepfather would try to make light of her story and poor old Caroline was too muddled to take it in. She wished that her husband might return soon, and the thought brought another. Perhaps it was just as well he was delayed since she might decide not to even take him into her confidence until she was sure of her facts. He would know something was wrong if he came and found her in this weak state. With despair she also realized she was allowing herself to be suspicious of him again, and condemned herself for it.

John Graham came back with two glasses of wine. He gave her one. "I need a wee drop myself," he said, and downed his drink.

Laura took a good swallow of the wine and let it trickle down. It warmed her at once and in a minute or two she began to feel better. "That does help," she announced with the pride of discovery.

"I need more," he said shortly, and left her for the sideboard again.

By the time he returned, carrying a bottle with him, she had finished her glass. She ventured, "We surely won't need all that."

He poured her another drink with grave care and then one for himself. As he raised his glass, he told her, "We'll judge the amount according to the speed of our recovery."

"I'm feeling better every minute," she declared after another warming swallow. "But I don't want Donald to come back and find us both sitting here drunk."

"Don't fret about that," he said with the hint of a Scotch burr showing in his pronunciation of "fret." "It takes a lot stronger liquid and more than a bottle of it to put me under the table."

"I haven't your capacity," she pointed out politely. And she took another sip of the wine. As it built up the already pleasant warmth within her, she said, "But actually I feel much better and distinctly sober."

"The shock," he stated brusquely. "You could drink the bottle alone and not know the effect until later. A few glasses of this sherry will do no more than restore your circulation after being out there on that damp grass."

"It was awful." She frowned at the memory of it as he refilled their glasses. She smiled at him. "You see how much wiser this is. We haven't upset any of the others and I'm improving every minute."

He nodded and studied her with stern eyes. "Would you mind explaining just what daft idea made you go out there alone in the dark?"

"I was tired of waiting for Donald. I thought I might see the lights of his car coming along the road. I wanted to surprise him by being there waiting for him."

He shook his head. "I have never heard such a fool idea."

She looked down at her half empty glass. "I guess it was stupid of me."

He grunted again and began to pace

back and forth in front of her. "When I met you and drove you both here from Glengarry the other day, I said to myself, 'He's married himself a pretty face and a trim figure but the girl hasn't an ounce of spirit and no hint of a brain!' "

"Indeed," she said with a faint recovery of indignation. "Is that what you thought of me. I was just beginning to like you."

"Don't!" he warned, halting in front of her. "I'm naturally an unpleasant person. People get on with me best when they accept me as I am."

Laura was perplexed by his brusque manner and blunt talk. Some Scotsmen were noted for this but it went further than that. Was John Graham jealous of her husband and acting this way because of it? She could accept this more readily than his explanation that he was an obnoxious person.

He eyed her. "Now I see you do have some spirit."

"And that's all?"

"That's all!"

"Thank you," she said. "Your understanding is beyond belief. Someone just tried to murder me and now you tell me I haven't a hint of a brain."

"I say it with due consideration," he

93

assured her as he paced again. "And I base it on your stupidity in going out there in the dark tonight. And on the fit of hysterics into which you worked yourself!"

"And why not?" she demanded in annoyance. "I had a right to hysterics. Someone tried to choke me with some kind of a cord!"

"More of your imaginings," he replied. "You've heard some sort of tale and now you're repeating it. There was no cord!"

"There was! We just didn't find it!"

He stood before her and shook his head. "No cord and no mark of it on your pretty throat when I examined it just now."

Her hand automatically raised to her neck. "But there has to be at least a chafe line," she insisted. "Even though the cord was tightened only a minute!"

The young man's face was grim. "Admit it, Mrs. Cameron. You got frightened and acted a little foolish."

Her blue eyes opened wide. "You mean after everything? After what you heard and saw yourself, you still don't believe me?"

He nodded. "You've said it exactly."

"Then it's you who is the fool!" she said, rising. "Or perhaps you have your own reasons for pretending that I imagined everything!"

John Graham showed amusement. "Such as?"

"It could have been you who attacked me," she said slowly. "It could easily have been you. I'm sure he looked like you."

The tall man chuckled. "I thought we'd get around to that." And then with disgust, "I should have let you stay there on the grass."

"Maybe you thought it would be wise to pretend to rescue me," she accused him. "To make sure that I didn't suspect you."

"And you've worked all that out on just three glasses of wine," John Graham marveled. "If I let you have the whole bottle you'd be able to tell a tale like Sir Walter Scott."

Laura was thoroughly angry now, and much of her fear and all of her faintness had vanished. "You're a nasty, sarcastic person," she said. "And I'm sorry I had to bother you."

He smiled mockingly and nodded. "No harm done. Just one thing I want to get straight before I leave you. Am I to mention this to your husband or not?"

"I'll tell my husband what I feel he should know," she replied with dignity. "And I'll thank you to keep your sarcastic tongue to yourself."

"That's what I wanted to find out," he said with urbane good humor. "I'll not say a word to him unless he mentions it to me first." He made his way to the reception hall and turned. "Goodnight, Mrs. Cameron, thanks for the entertainment." With another of his tormenting smiles he vanished.

She stared after him filled with mixed emotions; frustration at the way he had baited and tormented her with smart replies, shock that until this moment she hadn't realized the kind of person he was. She had taken him for a sullen, reticent person, interested only in his work, and just now he had shown her a completely opposite side of his character: assured, witty and possessed of undeniable animal magnetism. She realized with some dismay that, when he liked, John Graham could be a charmer. He could make a girl's head spin without too much effort.

She had found herself beginning to like him until he had taunted her. He had even done that in such a way that she couldn't be sure he meant it. She couldn't be sure of anything about him. It was even possible, although he had made it seem like a preposterous suggestion on her part, that he had been the one who had attacked her.

He was a good enough actor to play any part, and was brazen to the extent that he could carry through any wild scheme. Her mind was not made up about John Graham. Not at all!

But his leaving her had done one thing: left her open to growing fear again. Her eyes ran the length of the nearly dark living room and she fervently wished that Donald would get home soon. She glanced at her watch and saw that it was now well after nine. He was late. She crossed over to the reception hall and peered out the small window next to the door. Her hand touched her throat again. Perhaps John Graham had told the truth and no telltale marks remained of the cord to prove her story. But she knew the tightening coil had nearly shut off her breath and it would be futile to try and make her admit to anything else.

What had happened tonight had been carefully planned, and if she was not mistaken, carefully planned by someone within the thick stone walls of Cameron Castle. She would question Mrs. Basset about the windows in the morning and find out who occupied the room where the light had been turned on. These thoughts were in her mind when she saw the lights of Donald's car in the driveway and heard the swish of his car wheels on the gravel. She watched as the car went around to the back, the red taillights vanishing behind the house. Then she waited with growing anticipation. Her heart began to pound with excitement as she heard his steps coming back along the walk and up to the door. She ran into his arms as he stepped through the door.

He kissed her. "I had no idea you'd be right here waiting for me."

"It seems as if I've been waiting for ages," she sighed, her head pressed against him.

"I'm late," he admitted. "I'm sorry. I ran into some fog along the road and it slowed me down."

She stood back to study his face again. "You look tired." And he did. There was a lined weariness in his face.

"A busy day," he said. "I've a lot to tell you."

"I've been waiting to hear about it." She managed a smile and thought, No it couldn't have been him! He is wearing a tan coat and no hat. And though his face shows a worn expression, it does not have that distortion of sheer hatred that showed in that other one. It couldn't have been him!

But the doubt was there. Deep within her it would remain, a repulsive, fearsome thing that she wouldn't dare investigate in the light or presence of others. It was like a loathsome sore that she must keep concealed and which would nag her at moments when she was alone and most needed comfort. Yes, the doubt would remain until she learned the full truth about tonight, even though she wouldn't dare admit its existence even to herself.

"I'd like something warm to drink," he said. "A hot toddy. Come to the kitchen and help me prepare it while I tell you about what happened in Sydney."

She put the hateful suspicions to the back of her mind, and pretended so well to be relieved and satisfied at his just being home that in a real sense she convinced herself. The sheer terror of the early evening was forgotten in this induced mood of pleasant relaxation.

They sat together in the big, somewhat bleak kitchen, with a single, hanging bulb for light, like any two normal young married people. He was seated on the edge of the table, a smile on his face as he sipped the mug of toddy which they had prepared with much banter and mutual enjoyment. She sat in a chair close by, an adoring expression on her face as she eagerly listened to him. There was no hint of what thoughts might be hidden behind his relaxed, smiling features. Nor was there any clue to her terror, which lurked only slightly below the surface, and which made her studied performance a major theatrical achievement. Yet she knew his thoughts and her terror were real. They did exist!

His voice broke into her reverie. "You should have seen the banker's face when I passed him your check. It would have done you good."

"Then it's all settled. You don't have to worry about the house anymore?"

Donald nodded. "All the back debt is automatically squared off. It's up to John Graham and me now to keep us running in the black. And I know we can do it."

"I'm sure you can," she agreed.

He smiled and, putting down the empty mug, he rummaged in his pocket and brought out a long envelope and passed it over to her. "It's a legal agreement signed by me," he said. "In which I turn over half ownership in the estate to you in return for the payment of those debts."

She opened the papers without bothering to read them since her eyes were brimming with tears. "It's too much," she protested. "I didn't want this."

"You have it anyway," he said, quietly. "It was the only fair thing to do. One day, if I'm able to ever raise that much money and want to buy your share back, you can sell it to me."

"I'd willingly give it to you."

He smiled at her gently. "Let it stand as it is. Half of all my possessions are yours by law in any case. So let me make the gesture. It helps clear my conscience for taking the money from you."

It was a happier climax than she could have hoped for to an evening that had brought her to the brink of terror. In this warm mood of reunion with her husband, she was able to push her fears far in the background, knowing well that they would return again soon enough, but parched to enjoy this short period of pleasure. As they turned off the kitchen light and started up to their own room, she congratulated herself on not having alerted the whole household to the attack on her.

This way was better. Only John Graham knew her secret and she had no reason to think he would betray her confidence. This way the surface of their living in the grim stone house could continue unruffled. Meanwhile she would be alert to any clues that might point to her attacker and his motives.

The days that followed continued in a pleasant and normal fashion. Donald seemed to have completely recovered from his moody spells and was filled with a new enthusiasm. When Laura happened to find herself in company with him and John Graham, she found the estate manager polite and reserved. Once or twice she thought she saw a hint of cynical amusement in his eyes, but otherwise he was the model of discretion.

Anna and her stepfather played their usual roles in the household. Austin Cameron was absorbed with his work at the college and his after-hours task of preparing some publications in Gaelic. Anna had her own small red car and did a lot of driving when she wasn't at school. Laura didn't see much of her, but there was no question of Anna's hostility towards her, although Laura did everything she could to be friendly. Aunt Caroline moved through the dim corridors of the great house like a majestic, old ghost. Some days her mind was completely clear and on others she would be vague and mumble of past events and long dead relatives and friends, ignoring those around her.

Laura made some discreet inquiries of Mrs. Basset concerning the window that had shown a light during the moment when she was being attacked, and was let down to discover it was Aunt Caroline's room. It meant the light could not have had any special significance.

Laura gradually forgot the ugly incident when she had nearly lost her life. It was something she wanted to dismiss from her mind. So she tried to be content to live each day for itself. Yet there were times in the night when she awoke with a start and found herself trembling. She would lie there, staring up into the shadows and hearing the even breathing of her husband deep in sleep at her side, and know that the canker of fear still remained, waiting only for some new happening to cause it to flare up again.

Laura was upset by her discovery that Frank Cameron was Aunt Caroline's favorite. Aunt Caroline tolerated Donald but she really loved the afflicted Frank. Perhaps, Laura decided, this was because of Frank's humiliating defect of birth which left him so freakishly hairless, and also partly due to his having so much sadness in his marriage. Frank came again one evening to visit them, and when Laura accompanied him to the door, he revealed his worry about his wife's health.

"June doesn't seem to be making any progress," he said with a sigh, the oval, white face showing his concern. "Of course, this is exactly what the doctors have predicted." He smiled sadly at her. "And you haven't come to see us yet. She's been asking about you."

"I'll try to come soon," she promised, feeling guilty at her neglect.

"Perhaps this weekend," Frank suggested. "I'll be home all day Saturday. I know it would mean a great deal to my wife. Anna might bring you over if Donald is busy. She sometimes comes to see us on her day off from school."

Laura knew she couldn't count on Anna. "I'll find a way to get there. I must get a car of my own soon. And a license so I can at least drive Donald's car."

Frank nodded his completely bald head. "That would be wise," he agreed.

When Donald's brother had driven away, she returned to the living room where Aunt Caroline was seated in her favorite easy chair by the fireplace. The proud old head raised as Laura entered and the still bright, blue eyes fixed on her.

"Frank is a fine young man," she said.

"He has never given any of us a moment of trouble. And life has been very cruel to him."

Laura sat by her and felt she understood what she meant. "I agree, he is a very nice person. And his wife's illness must be a great burden. But Donald has many problems as well. The estate has been a drag on him," she defended her husband.

Aunt Caroline shrugged and looked into the fire. "Frank would have done well if he'd been the first son and inherited Cameron Castle. Perhaps even better than Donald."

So there it was! Aunt Caroline was prejudiced in Frank's favor and Laura began to suspect that there might be some definite reason for her firm convictions. She had the uneasy feeling that the old woman's judgment was influenced by facts of which she was not aware. Unpleasant truths concerning her husband. And again she immediately berated herself for so easily doubting him.

Every so often he did something really touching that made her love for him increase. Not necessarily important acts, but ones that showed his thoughtful, sensitive nature. On Friday evening she was reminded of this side of his character when he returned from the village with a small parcel for her. He brought it up to the room where she was doing some final touches on her hair before preparing to go down to dinner.

Coming toward the dresser, he smiled at her in the mirror and leaned down to give her the neat parcel. "Open it," he said. "It's meant to be a guide for you."

She removed the twine and paper to reveal a pretty little Highland doll dressed in plaid kilt, dark jacket, tam, and all the decorations of the native Scottish garb. The doll even had her blonde hair and blue eyes.

"It's wonderful, darling!" she exclaimed, glancing up at him over her shoulder. "Where did you get it?"

He touched his lips to her hair. "There is a crafts shop in the village. They make these dolls with authentic costumes for the tourist trade. I wanted you to have one so you could get an idea of the way you must dress for the Highland Gathering we have here in June."

She studied the doll with affection. "I'll try to get an outfit just like this. I think she's beautiful."

Laura was so delighted with her gift that she took it down to dinner and showed it to the others. Even Anna had something nice to say about it. And Austin Cameron was enthusiastic.

"The crafts shop should make more of them and ship them far and wide. Cape Breton should capitalize on the way of life we've preserved."

Aunt Caroline then delighted him by offering a few words in Gaelic, which she later told Laura meant she thoroughly approved of his suggestion. When dinner was over, Anna came to her.

"I'm going to visit Frank and his wife tomorrow," she said. "I'll be stopping by another friend's place as well. But you could stay there and I'll pick you up on my way back."

"I'd like to go, unless Donald has some plans," Laura said, pleased that the girl should be suddenly so friendly to her.

Anna's lovely face showed a veiled expression. "I doubt if he'll ever want to take you there. You can ask him if you like."

"I will," she promised, puzzled by the other girl's words and determined to question her husband on the matter. What possible reason could Donald have for not wanting to take her to his brother's cottage?

CHAPTER FIVE

After taking the doll upstairs and placing it on the dresser, Laura went down to the lower level of the old castle and sought out Donald in his study. He greeted her with a smile and invited her to sit down.

"I didn't mean to interfere with your work," she apologized.

"Nothing important," he assured her, sitting back and filling his long-stemmed pipe from a leather tobacco pouch. "It's just a list of a cattle sale that is being held in Finlayson tomorrow. Graham and I plan to attend. We think we might pick up some good stock at reasonable prices."

"I see," she said, with a little sigh. "The weather is so nice, I was hoping we might take a drive together tomorrow afternoon."

"Saturday is the big day for cattle auctions," he explained. "Of course you're welcome to come along if you like."

"I don't think so," she said. She was anxious to tell him of Anna's offer to take her to Frank's. And she was determined to ask him whether he might prefer to take her and share this first visit to her ailing sister-in-law.

"If the weather is fine on Sunday we could take a drive up toward the Cabot Trail," he suggested. "We might go as far as Cape Smoky and drive over its crown. To drive up there, with its frequent cloud-caps, is a real thrill."

"I'd like that," she agreed. "Anna offered to drive me over to visit Frank and his wife tomorrow."

He touched a match to his filled pipe, took a few puffs, and tossed the match in the desk ashtray. He stared at her for a moment in silence, his handsome face very sober now. "That might be a good idea," he said at last. "It would fill in your day while I'm at the cattle auction."

She felt that the plan pleased him. He seemed actually relieved at her suggestion, and she began to wonder if he had been behind Anna's invitation. Anna had seemed very sure of herself, and it was all very odd.

"That is true. But it seems to me that it might be nicer if we went together on my first visit to meet June."

He looked down at his desk, avoiding her eyes. "I don't think that is so important."

At once a doubt began to form in her

mind. He was behaving exactly as Anna had predicted. She began to feel the old fear coming back, to feel that she had never properly understood him.

"I'd feel better if you were with me. And don't you think Frank and his wife would appreciate it?"

He took his pipe from his mouth. "I doubt it," he said dryly.

"I've been here quite awhile and we've never gone to visit them. I don't want them to feel slighted."

With a shrug he lifted his eyes to meet hers and too casually said, "Then I think this offer of Anna's is ideal. Go over with her tomorrow."

Laura hesitated, staring at him with perplexed eyes. "Why couldn't we both go together on Sunday? Postponing the visit a day wouldn't matter."

"I think the weather will be good on Sunday," he said. "It would be an ideal time to take you up to the National Park and the Cabot Trail."

"I see," she said slowly. "What you're trying to tell me in so many words is, you have no intention of going to Frank's with me any day."

Her husband's face showed surprise, and then faint annoyance. "I think you're making a great deal out of nothing."

"Is that or is that not true?" she persisted.

He got up, and moving across to the bay window, stared out at the brilliant red sunset. "You'd better go with Anna," he said shortly, his back to her.

Now she stood up. "If you won't go to your brother's, there must be some reason," she said. "Why make such a mystery of it?"

"It is you who are making the mystery," he accused, his back still to her.

She stared at this tall, handsome man whom she had married in such haste. Once again she was reminded that in many ways they were still strangers; that she knew less about him than probably anyone else in the old house. Did he enjoy making her feel like an outsider? Humiliating her in this fashion! She had hoped that when she'd cleared off the estate's debt that there would be no other barriers to their happiness, but she should have known differently. Aunt Alice's harsh predictions rang in her ears again.

And she should have guessed from Anna's friendly offer, and from her mocking smile when she'd suggested that Donald would not be anxious to visit

Frank's cottage, that there was some hidden reason of which she was unaware.

With a note of defiance in her voice, she said, "I'm sick of your weak alibis and subterfuges whenever it suits you. I'm tired of all this village secrecy and concealed motives not understandable to outsiders! Do you enjoy shutting me out of your life?"

"Let's not quarrel about it, Laura," he said with utter weariness, his eyes still on the fading sunset.

She weakened a little at his words. "I have no wish to quarrel," she replied. "But I do wish you trusted me more."

He turned to her quickly, and with sober face said, "I think it's you who shows no trust. You don't seem to have any faith in me at all. I'd like to see a different attitude in my wife."

She was cut deeply by his quiet words. All the worse because she knew there was more than a grain of truth in them. Laura had a desperate impulse to blurt out the things she had kept from him; to tell him about the attack on her and how the face of her attacker had seemed for a moment to be his. But she rapidly decided against it, sensing that it would not help at all and perhaps would make everything more difficult. This was something she must suffer alone.

She lowered her head and very quietly apologized. "I'm sorry, Donald."

He came over to her and touched a hand to her arm. "Earlier tonight it seemed to me we were ideally happy," he said. "Why must these misunderstandings always follow?"

Laura shook her head, her eyes on the carpet. "Perhaps we made a mistake. We rushed into marriage so quickly. It could be we are wrong for each other."

"I won't accept that."

"It happens," she said tautly. "Why should we rule it out in our case? You won't ever be completely frank with me. And it seems to be my nature to always doubt you."

"I thought you understood," he said. "I happen to be a complex person. I'm afraid I can't change that. Call me a dour Scot if you want. I thought you were satisfied to accept me as I am."

"I want us to be happy," she said, looking up into his troubled face.

"Then don't always demand instant explanations," he warned her. "Some things are best discovered slowly and in their proper time. Don't be so ready to condemn my actions at every turn."

They stood facing each other in the silence of the small room. Then at last, she promised, "I'll try, Donald. I'll try very hard."

The discussion ended without anything being settled. Again she lay awake in the darkness and wondered about the man she had married; this quiet Scot who put such emphasis on the trust she should show in him and who seemed reluctant to place any in her. He had brought her to this huge, sinister old house with its assortment of his hostile relatives, and expected her to be happy, happy in this rugged, isolated tip of the continent where many of the people spoke in the ancient Gaelic that she could not even understand. Ought he to have married Anna? Would it have been better? She fell asleep with this bitter thought.

Saturday was another lovely day and Donald left early with John Graham to attend the cattle auction at Finlayson. Laura, insisting on her plan to take on her share of the housework, spent most of the morning cleaning their room and changing bedclothes. Only when she had done all these tasks to her satisfaction did she go downstairs. It was getting near noon and she discovered Aunt Caroline out in the sun porch enjoying the fresh spring air and sunshine.

Aunt Caroline glanced up at her. "Your man has gone to Finlayson," she said.

"Yes. He thinks there might be some bargains in stock there."

Aunt Caroline pointed her cane toward the barns which could be seen from the porch. "Cameron Castle has always had the best of prize cattle," she said. "His father won't let him buy any that don't fit the standard."

Laura realized the old woman's mind was wandering again. She said, "I'm sure Graham will give him good advice." It was an attempt to guide her back to reality.

Aunt Caroline's eyes were glazed as she continued to stare at the distant gray barns. In a thin voice she said, "In Skye they used to catch a bumblebee. Catch a bumblebee in spring and put it in your purse and you are sure not to be out of money until another spring. And on Islay a horse's ears were stuffed with butter on the first day of the ploughing season. And heather was burned to make sure of rain and that the harvest would be bountiful. The blossoming of a white rose means an early death and the red rose an early marriage. And my man was from the Hebrides and before he took the cattle off pasture and housed them for the winter, fire was carried round them three times, sunways." The old lady lapsed into silence, her eyelids dropping closed, and she sank back in the chair.

Laura withdrew from the porch quietly, knowing a short nap would do a great deal of good for Aunt Caroline. Likely she would be her usual alert self when she woke up.

After lunch Laura went to her room and changed into a dark blue silk dress, suitable for afternoon visiting. She had just finished at the dresser mirror and was taking her topcoat from the closet when there was a knock on her door.

It was Anna Gordon. She smiled. "So you've decided to come with me?"

"Yes," Laura said very casually. "With Donald away it seemed a good time to go."

Anna's glance was knowing. "I thought he'd approve," she said.

Laura had an idea the girl wanted to worry the subject over again to discover how much Laura had found out. She had no intention of giving Anna that satisfaction. It was humiliating enough to discover her prediction had been right without having to admit it.

Anna proved to be a good driver as they made their way along the winding dirt road that connected the various buildings on the estate. She gave Laura a glance.

"I'm glad you've come," she said. "I don't think you're going to believe me, but I'd like us to be friends."

Laura gave a small laugh. "I don't know any reason why we shouldn't be."

"You know plenty," Anna assured her with sharp humor. "But let's try to forget about them."

"That sounds realistic and practical," Laura admitted.

"We are living in the same house," Anna went on, "and whatever our differences of opinion, we surely agree on one thing. We are both on Donald's side."

"I certainly hope that I am," she said, somewhat taken back at the girl's statements.

They drove through gently rolling fields with the inevitable evergreens and blue mountains in the background. Then they suddenly hit a down grade, rounded a turn, and there appeared a picture-book cottage with shuttered windows and colorful shingled roof in the same light red as the shutters. The cottage itself was painted white. A garage stood in the rear of it, reached by its own short piece of road, and a blue sedan, which Laura recognized as belonging to Frank, was parked there.

"Looks as though everyone is home," Anna said as she braked the little red sedan to a stop in front of the attractive cottage.

"It's an ideal place," Laura said, thinking how much she would prefer such a house for Donald and her.

"Frank built it about five years ago after the original place burned down," Anna related. "I was away at college at the time but I believe his wife almost lost her life in the blaze. She was sick even then. Frank was away on a court case in Sydney but luckily John Graham happened to be driving by and saw smoke. He saved her."

"I hadn't heard about it," she confessed, realizing it was only one of many things about which she was uninformed.

"The original cottage was very old," Anna said as they got out of the car. "I guess the wiring was faulty or something of the sort. They never did find out."

Laura remembered and asked, "Will you be leaving me here alone for a while when you go on to visit your other friend?"

Anna nodded. "Yes. I hope you don't mind. I won't be long."

"Of course not," she said. "It will give me a chance to get acquainted with June."

The mocking look came into the girl's lovely face again. "Exactly," she said.

Frank Cameron opened the door to them and the expression of pleasure on his big pink and white face repaid them for taking the trouble to make the call.

"Come in," he begged. "How wonderful to see you both!" His glowing enthusiasm continued as he sat with them a moment in the living room before taking them in to see his invalid wife.

"I'm glad you decided to come today," Frank said. "June is having one of her good days. She is much better than usual."

"I can't stay long," Anna told him. "I have to make another call. But I'll come back as soon as I can."

"Excellent." Frank nodded his head approvingly. "That means Laura will be having a nice long visit with us."

"That is what I thought," Anna agreed.

Frank rose to take them into his wife's sickroom. In a low voice he said, "June is not more than three or four years older than you, Laura. But her illness has aged her. Please don't be shocked by her appearance."

Laura thought the invalid looked reasonably well, aside from the fact she was deathly pale and emaciated. Her auburn hair had been neatly arranged and she was propped up against pillows. She smiled as her husband led them into the room. She had small features and must have been pretty once, but now her large green eyes were set in dark hollows. She greeted Anna in a friendly way, and when Frank introduced Laura, gave her a warm welcome.

June Cameron held out a thin hand and took Laura's in it. There was a clammy moistness to her touch that repulsed Laura. She tried hard to mask her feelings as she bent to kiss her sister-in-law. June insisted she take a chair at her bedside, and then stared at her in mild wonderment.

"You're younger and more attractive than I expected," she said. "But then Frank is no good at describing people."

After a few minutes Anna excused herself and Frank went with her to see her safely on her way. Laura found herself alone with June Cameron, and feeling more than a little awkward.

Then June said, "I do hope you're going to be happy here."

"I'm gradually getting adjusted. It's a little difficult."

"Naturally. This is a foreign land and a

very different section of it at that."

"I know little about the area," Laura went on. "I've really met no one aside from those at the castle."

"It's high time you did."

She smiled. "I'm sure Donald will gradually introduce me to everyone. But I felt I couldn't put off meeting you any longer."

"I'm glad you felt that way."

There had been no hint offered why Donald might not have been expected to accompany her. Laura's curiosity was increasing. She ventured, "I was going to wait until Donald could come with me."

The thin woman, hunched against her pillows and looking directly at Laura, said in her whining sick person's tone, "That wouldn't have been wise!"

Laura tried to restrain any show of surprise. "No?" she asked politely.

"Your husband won't come to see me."

She had expected this reply and was ready with her response. "Why on earth not?"

June Cameron hesitated, her pale face drawn. She turned and stared out the window. "We had a serious argument one day. I said some things. I don't think he'll ever forgive me."

"But that's ridiculous!" Laura exclaimed. At the same time she felt her old fear coming back, recognizing that such an attitude would be possible with her husband. He could be stiff and unrelenting as he'd shown himself to her on more than one occasion.

"Things were said that neither of us would want to take back," the sick woman went on, still looking away.

"But he and Frank are brothers, and with you ill as you are, I'm sure he should have shown you more consideration," Laura insisted, realizing she still didn't have a hint as to what the quarrel might have been about.

Now June turned to stare at her again, her sunken eyes troubled. "Perhaps I was the offender. Maybe I shouldn't have said what I did to him."

Laura frowned. "You make it sound like something monstrous," she said in a low voice.

There was a moment of silence in the sickroom. A moment in which Laura was very conscious of being alone with this near stranger. She wished that Frank would soon show himself and wondered where he had gone.

June looked directly at her. "I told your husband I thought he was a murderer," she said very evenly.

The shock, all the more so because of the quiet way in which June Cameron had made her statement, hit Laura full force and left her staring speechless at her sister-in-law. She felt her head reel dizzily as she frantically tried to regain her composure. She had expected to hear something unpleasant but nothing as bad as this.

"Do you realize what you said?" she asked in a hollow voice.

"I'm sorry," June Cameron apologized. "I feel for you deeply. You are in no way to blame for any of it."

Laura swallowed hard. No wonder Donald had refused to come to this house. It was understandable that he objected to visiting this woman who considered him a criminal of the most despicable type. But on what were her accusations based? And why hadn't Donald frankly explained the situation to her, since it seemed clear everyone else in the area must know the details. Certainly Anna did. That was why she had arranged this meeting with June Cameron and herself in the first place and why she had gloated so.

"It is my problem though," Laura said, finding her voice again. "It does concern my husband."

"And you are deeply devoted to him?"

"Of course, I love him."

June's white face wore a stricken look. "I didn't mean to tell you," she said in a despairing voice. "I'm a weak, silly woman."

"Didn't mean to tell her what?" Frank Cameron asked sharply as he strode into the room and stood at the foot of his sick wife's bed with a troubled look on his broad face.

June stared at him and fingered the coverlet nervously. "It just came out, Frank. I told her about Donald."

"No!" He let the word explode from him. He turned to stare at Laura with a sickly expression. "And you hadn't heard anything about it before?"

"Not a word," Laura said.

"That's terrible!" Frank shook his head. "I'd have given anything for you not to have heard it from us." Then his eyes narrowed. "Do you actually mean to say Donald didn't discuss this with you before you were married? Before he brought you here to live?"

"I still don't know what you're talking about," she said in a harried tone. "Your wife has accused Donald of being a murderer, but I don't know why."

"You see the sort of person he is," June Cameron told her husband.

Frank seemed stunned. He ran a hand over his bald pate and looking at Laura again, said, "It's just incredible!"

On the edge of desperation she leaned forward in her chair and begged him, "Please stop talking around it and tell me the facts I should know."

There was another poignant pause and then June motioned wearily to her husband. "Go ahead, Frank. She's heard this much, she deserves to know the rest."

He seemed dazed. He took a few steps toward the window and looked out. Then, as if resolving himself to go on with the ordeal, he turned and addressed himself to Laura.

"It goes back two years ago," he said slowly. "Donald was seeing a good deal of a girl in the village. The daughter of a well-to-do lumberman, Fiona Sutherland. Fiona was June's best friend and a regular visitor here."

"The poor dear came to see me twice a week at least," June whimpered.

"She was a fine girl and a beautiful one, with all the education and advantages to appeal to someone like Donald," his brother went on. "I, for one, thought it

125

would be a match. So did most of the people around here." He paused and his face became grim. "Of course, there was a shadow that spoiled it all."

"It was him!" June Cameron said in a grief-stricken voice. "He has never been trustworthy."

"Donald and Fiona had a quarrel because she thought he was too friendly with another girl in the village, a married woman to be exact." He gave Laura an inquiring glance. "You've heard of his friends Glenna and David MacGregor?"

"Yes," she said in little more than a whisper.

"Fiona thought he was more friendly than he should be with Glenna Mac-Gregor. The poor girl came to us with the whole story. She was heartbroken."

"But what about this Glenna Mac-Gregor's husband," Laura said. "I thought he and Donald were friends?"

"They are still supposed to be," June Cameron jeered. "Donald has pulled the wool over David's eyes for ages. The poor fool believes everything that is told him by Glenna and Donald. And he's a drinker! A heavy one. A good deal of the time he doesn't know what is going on around him."

Frank sighed from his stand near the window. "That's about the truth of it. Had David MacGregor been the proper kind of husband none of this would have happened. There would have been no tragedy and Fiona might be alive today."

June Cameron murmured. "He killed her in a spiteful rage because she refused to go back with him, and I told him so to his face."

Frank shrugged. "You can't be sure, you know. The authorities aren't. Or Donald would have been hung for the killing long before this. All they know is that he was the last person anyone saw her with. They found her body in a lover's lane parking spot just before midnight. The Mounted Police put the murder down as being committed between nine and eleven."

"And the first person the Mounties suspected was Donald Cameron!" June said vindictively.

Frank looked unhappy. "Again, that doesn't count for too much. When the Mounted Police questioned around, they soon discovered the relationship between Donald and Fiona. And they produced several witnesses who said they had seen them talking near Donald's car on the main street of the village that night."

"But that is all circumstantial evidence!" she protested.

Frank nodded. "So the authorities decided. Meanwhile my brother was put through a lot of questioning. He denied all knowledge of the crime, and many in the area, including Fiona's father, felt he was telling the truth."

"And a lot thought him guilty and still do," June Cameron put in.

"That is so," her husband said. "Unfortunately for Donald. He was cleared of the crime by the authorities but since Fiona's murder has never been solved, many of the folk in the district feel he was the one who did it."

"I can see that," Laura said with difficulty. "I still don't think he could be a murderer."

"And I agree," Frank Cameron said with finality. He glanced at his wife. "June and I differ on very few matters. But this is a point of violent disagreement between us. I believe my brother to be innocent and she doesn't."

"I never will," the sick woman said stubbornly. "Fiona was my closest friend."

"I can understand your feelings," Laura said in a quiet voice, trying to hide the fact that she was on the verge of an emotional collapse. "I'm sorry my coming here brought all this up."

"I think Donald has been very wrong in hiding this from you," Frank said in genuine distress. "I suppose he was afraid that if you heard the story you wouldn't marry him."

"Perhaps that was it," she agreed weakly.

"A weakling's reason," was June Cameron's scornful comment. "As least he should have been honest with you."

"I must agree on that." Frank Cameron's pink, hairless face was agitated. "To bring you here in ignorance this way was most regrettable. Perhaps it is just as well the subject came up here today. It would be an agonizing experience for you to hear such a story from strangers."

Laura felt like telling him it was an agonizing experience to hear it at all. But she could see that June was upset from the ordeal of the long, difficult conversation, and Frank Cameron was in a highly tense state himself.

She got up from the chair. "I must go now," she said.

Frank looked startled. "But you can't until Anna returns with the car."

"She'll be along soon and I don't want to keep her waiting," Laura improvised desperately. "I'll watch for her from the front steps. I need some fresh air." She turned to the woman in the bed. "Again I'm sorry for putting you through this."

June Cameron's eyes were closed in utter weariness, she looked corpselike. "Doesn't matter," she murmured. "Come again."

"I will," Laura promised. "Later." Not at all sure that she could ever force herself to return to this room with the unhappy memories it would always have for her, but striving to maintain at least a pretense of calmness.

A worried Frank saw her to the front door. "You don't have to pretend with me," he said. "I know exactly how you must feel, and you have my deepest sympathy."

She sighed. "At least you feel Donald was blamed wrongly."

"As you yourself pointed out, the evidence was purely circumstantial. I feel I know my own brother as well as anyone and I agree he could never be a murderer. My wife is prejudiced because she thought so much of Fiona. It's all a very sad and awkward business."

They were standing on the cottage steps. There was still no sign of Anna's red car. She looked at him. "Of course they all know at the castle. Even Aunt Caroline, I suppose."

He nodded gravely. "Even Aunt Caroline. I'm afraid it upset the poor old girl a great deal. She is very sensitive about the family name and she has never forgiven Donald, I fear."

Laura had sensed the hidden antagonism in the old woman all along. And now she knew the reason for it. Understood why she had turned to Frank as her favorite. She said, "And yet none of them ever spoke to me of it."

"They probably thought my brother had told you. And they wouldn't want to bring it up. Naturally they wouldn't want to hurt your feelings."

She stared off in the distance. "I believe Anna guessed the truth. That I didn't know. That is why she wanted me to come here today."

"Surely not," he brushed aside the suggestion. "She knew you wanted to meet my wife and made it easy for you."

"Very easy," she agreed grimly. Then, as a new question came to mind, she looked at him and asked, "How was this girl killed?"

Frank sighed. "She was strangled. A cord was used. A cord the murderer gradually tightened about her neck."

CHAPTER SIX

Laura closed her eyes for a brief moment as she heard this description of the murder method. It brought her shock and fear to a new peak. Even before he had told her, she had been almost certain that was what he would say. It all fitted in.

She heard Frank Cameron anxiously ask, "You're not going to faint?"

Opening her eyes again, she shook her head slowly. "No," she murmured. "I'll be all right." She strived to maintain a calm she did not feel. It was a lovely spring afternoon, with the sun warm and the air filled with the promise of blossoming growth; an afternoon in which one rejoiced to be alive. She had come here to visit the sick and enjoy a quiet conversation. It should have been a pleasant, relaxing time.

Instead it had turned into a nightmare! She had been exposed to a series of damning facts about her husband that taxed her imagination. It seemed she could not summon the strength to cope with this monstrous reality that had been revealed to her. She was married to a man who might be a murderer. Someone who was still looked on as a probable killer by many of the people around them. Worst of all he had kept this from her, allowing her to marry him and come here innocently. And already her own life had been in jeopardy!

Against the advice of her friends and her only relative, Aunt Alice, she had not only married Donald Cameron, but blithely proceeded to make him the beneficiary to her not inconsiderable fortune, should anything happen to her. She had been warned and it was working out exactly along the lines of these dire predictions. Already he had allowed her to pay off the estate's debts, but she was sure that would not be enough. He would become greedy for more money, anxious to be rid of her! And then!

Frank said urgently again, "You look deathly ill. Won't you please come inside and sit down until Anna arrives?"

"I'm better out here in the air."

Frank sighed. "I feel responsible for this. I don't know what to say. I can only plead forgiveness on the score of June being such a sick woman. I don't think she would have so callously revealed all this if she wasn't in such a dreadful state."

Laura turned to the unhappy man and saw the look of deep regret on the odd pink-skinned face. "I had to hear it sooner or later. Better, as you pointed out, that it come from within the family."

He moistened his lips nervously. "You mustn't let this change your feelings toward Donald. Don't allow your emotions to cause you to act before you have thought this all out."

She offered him an ironical smile. "Your advice is good, but under the circumstances it won't be easy to follow."

"We've both agreed that Donald was innocent," Frank went on quickly. "That is the most important thing to keep in mind."

"But no one can ever be sure unless the real murderer is revealed," she pointed out.

He looked distressed. "The police were very thorough in their investigations but didn't seem to get anywhere. I'm afraid the possibility of the case actually being solved is extremely unlikely now." He spread his hands. "What it amounts to is, the people close to Donald, the people who really believe in him, must accept his innocence as a matter of faith."

She stared hard at the earnest face, the troubled eyes so weirdly alive without a vestige of brows or lashes, like plastic fixtures installed in the recesses of pink flesh. And she felt an immediate sympathy for this man, who had borne his strange affliction all his life, who had been given the additional trial of an invalid wife, and who was trying now to cope with the shadow of guilt hovering over his brother.

Her concern for his feelings helped her regain some of her own composure. She said, "I understand. I'll try to deal with this sensibly."

"I know I can depend on you," he said in a grateful voice.

"And you mustn't blame either yourself or June for my finding out," she went on. "I surely am not angry at either of you."

The understanding between them might have been developed even more had Anna's car not appeared over the crest of the hill at that moment. Laura bid Frank a hurried good-bye and went out to stand by the roadside until Anna brought the car to a halt before her.

If Anna thought there was anything strange about her and Frank both being out on the steps waiting, she did not show it. She leaned over the wheel to wave a passing greeting at him as Laura got into the car beside her. Frank returned the greeting and stood watching after them as they drove on.

Anna seemed in a brisk good humor. "I didn't keep you waiting too long, did I?"

"No," Laura answered absently, her eyes turned to the window as she took in the passing panorama of green fields, evergreens and occasional huge boulders that marked the rugged country.

"Did you have a pleasant visit? June is very nice in spite of her illness. I think she bears up remarkably."

"Yes," Laura replied in a toneless voice again, her thoughts far distant.

"Is something wrong? You sound upset."

Laura turned to her. "I think you know. They told me."

"Told you?" Anna pitched her words casually, but from the tense expression showing on her face, Laura was sure that she knew, that she had hoped and expected it would happen.

"About Fiona Sutherland's murder and Donald being suspected of it."

Anna's face drained of color, she kept busy at the wheel, her eyes fixed on the narrow dirt road ahead. "That," she said. "But didn't he tell you about all that long ago? I mean, before you were married."

"No."

"That never occurred to me."

"I wonder," Laura said quietly. "You were very eager for me to come here this afternoon. It seems to me you wanted me to find out this way."

"You're being ridiculous."

"Have it your own way," Laura said, glancing out the window. She had been on the point of bringing her thoughts out into the open, accusing Anna of being in love with Donald, asking why she hadn't married him. But she decided to keep silent.

Anna's face was shadowed with anger as she drove on. "I don't enjoy being called a sly schemer," she said.

"Well, now the story is out whether you planned it or not."

"And?"

"And I'm faced with the fact that I may have married a murderer."

The girl at the wheel gave her a scornful glance. "If you really believe that you shouldn't have married Don in the first place."

Looking at her, Laura could see more surely than ever before that Anna was in love with her husband. No need to put it in words. It was an unspoken fact between them.

Very evenly she replied, "I only stated

the fact. I didn't give any hint of what I might believe."

"I know by the way you spoke," Anna retorted hotly. "You've convicted him in your mind already."

"That's not true!"

The girl drove on in silence for a few minutes. Then she asked, "Now that you do know, what are you going to do about it?"

Laura leaned back against the seat and closed her eyes. "I haven't been able to think about it yet."

"If you love Don it won't make any difference!"

"I didn't say that it would."

"But I can tell by your manner that it will," Anna argued on. "You're going to bring it all up again. Make him go through new torture needlessly. You aren't woman enough to be silent about it. To let it rest!"

She opened her eyes and stared at the flushed profile of the girl at the wheel. "How can you say such things?" she asked quietly. "How dare you judge me so casually?"

"I know your husband is not a murderer or a cheat. Apparently you think he may be both!"

Laura said, "I love him. Isn't that enough?"

"With you, I wonder," Anna said bitterly. "I can't picture you defending him. I suppose you let June say all kinds of terrible things about him and never opened your mouth in his defense!"

"I didn't know what she was talking about at first. After I found out, I was too stunned to say much," she explained. "But that doesn't mean I agreed with all that she had told me."

"Silence gives consent," Anna said grimly.

"One thing I do know. He should have told me himself. I should have known before I came here." Laura was actually thinking aloud.

"He probably knew you well enough to be certain you'd run from him like a timid rabbit," Anna said with obvious disgust.

Laura looked at her angry face. "I'm not a timid rabbit. Neither am I a silly one. I think Donald made a mistake in that, and I wouldn't be afraid to tell him so."

Anna brought the car to a halt at the rear of the castle. "Since we live here under the same roof I'll try to forget this talk ever took place. And I think you'd be wise to do the same. At least for the sake of the others we can make a show of still being friends!"

The final, bitter words said, Anna

quickly got out of the car and slammed the door after her. Still sitting there, Laura watched her stride toward the rear entrance of the castle. Anna's words had hit her with a shocking impact, but in a way they had done her some good. She realized that she had been on the edge of really breaking up and the girl's words had brought her back to the point where she could consider her problem with some kind of objectivity. She sighed, opened the car door, and got out, feeling completely exhausted.

The afternoon was becoming cooler as the sun lost its strength, and as she stood in the yard for a moment, she noticed for the first time that their car was there. This meant John Graham and Donald must have returned from the cattle auction. She guessed they must be in the barn. Graham had an office there in which he kept all the farm's records. She hurried across the yard and up the wooden rise leading to the wide blackness of the open barn door.

Inside its shadowed interior she was aware of the pungent, but not unpleasant, barn smells. She saw no one and so made her way along the short passage that led to Graham's tiny office. She found the door open and Graham standing by the high built-in desk. The estate manager turned to her with a friendly expression on his tanned face that so resembled Donald's.

"You don't call on me often enough," he said with a smile.

Ignoring this, she asked, "Where is my husband?"

His brow furrowed. "You sound like it's an emergency. Is the castle on fire or has somebody tried to attack you again?"

Laura was indignant. "I don't find your remarks funny."

"You're much too serious a lass for Highland country," John Graham said, his Scot's burr in evidence now. "You needn't worry about your husband. He remained behind to have dinner with one of the dealers who'll drive him here later."

"That's the information I wanted," she said, and turned to leave.

"Mrs. Cameron!" he called after her.

She hesitated, frowning at him. "Yes?"

A disarming twinkle showed in his brown eyes. "I meant no harm. I'm afraid my country way of joking upset you."

"You are right," she said evenly.

John Graham looked puzzled. "I don't understand it," he said slowly. "You're not yourself at all. What has happened to upset you? If you're worried about my saying anything about the other night, I can promise I've never mentioned it to a soul. And that includes your husband. I did exactly as you asked."

She saw that he was sincere and realized that she had probably been unduly short with him because of her own agitation. Actually he had proved by his silence that he was her friend and someone on whom she could perhaps depend in this bewildering new land in which she found herself.

"I appreciate that," she said. "And I didn't mean to sound angry. The truth is, something has upset me."

"That's obvious."

Looking at him directly, she burst out, "For the first time today I learned that Donald was suspected of a murder."

Graham looked surprised. "I thought you knew," he said quietly.

"I suppose so," she said with some bitterness. "And that's why you came to the conclusion I imagined that attack the other night. You assumed I would be in an unduly nervous frame of mind."

"Something like that."

"Well, now you know different."

The estate manager shrugged. "I don't see why you should let it bother you so. The authorities didn't press any charges

142

against your husband. If they decided he wasn't guilty, why should you worry?"

"It wasn't pleasant news to hear."

"I can well imagine that," he said. "Donald should have told you. Maybe he wanted to spare you the shock of it. It was natural that he be questioned. He kept company with Fiona for a time."

"So I heard."

John Graham's face clouded. "I warned him against her. I told him she was a sly one. The sort that couldn't be true to any one man. He didn't listen to me in the beginning. But he found out for himself and broke with her before she was murdered."

Laura found this new light on the past of engrossing interest. She stared at John Graham. "I thought this Fiona was a wonderful person; lovely, well-educated and wealthy."

"She was all those things," Graham agreed sadly. "But she was more. Fiona was a heartless little flirt. As a wife she'd have broken the heart and spirit of any decent man."

"I see," she said, her thoughts racing at his words. If what Graham said was true, it was likely the murdered girl must have made many enemies. No doubt the local authorities had been aware of that, and it explained why they had been so ready to dismiss the idea that Donald had killed her, even though he had been the last to be seen in her company that evening.

Perhaps Anna had come close to the truth when she accused her of not loving her husband enough to have faith in him. Frank had said the same thing, in a different way. Now she began to feel less tense and somewhat ashamed. As usual, she had been too ready to blame Donald. But there had been the attack on her the other night. Who had been guilty of that? Perhaps whoever had strangled Fiona had tried to murder her in the same way so that suspicion would fall on Donald for both crimes. Yet, she had caught a glimpse of her attacker and he had resembled Donald to a startling degree. She raised her eyes to study John Graham's face, and again was struck by his close likeness to her husband.

Once before she had questioned whether her attacker had been Graham. Now the suspicion occurred again in a way that was vivid and frightening. She was suddenly conscious of being alone with him here in this remote part of the large barn.

He studied her with grave eyes. "I'd let the matter rest," he advised. "You go on turning up stones and you're going to find something unpleasant."

"I suppose so," she said reluctantly.

"We did all right at the auction," Graham went on. "Donald picked up some good cattle. Don't spoil the day for him with this when he comes back."

She gave him a bitter smile. "What about my day?"

"I know it hasn't been pleasant. But remember, it's been a lot worse for him. He loved that girl once, and he's had to live with the shadow of her murder for a long time."

She saw the truth in his serious words and yet she wondered. Was he telling her this to make sure she wouldn't raise any fuss, making the murder a current problem again and perhaps finally turning the spotlight on himself. It was a possibility she couldn't overlook.

"I'll keep that in mind," she promised.

The estate manager nodded. "He's a quiet, dour man and not given to easy talk any more than I am. But he loves you, Mrs. Cameron. Don't you fret about that."

"Thank you," she said quietly.

An amused look came to his tanned face again. "Which, of course, is too bad since I take a deep interest in you myself. Should the field be clear, I'd be the first to make my offer."

"That's another of your jokes I'm not liable to understand or approve of," she said without a smile. "Thank you for your information and advice, Mr. Graham." And she went quickly on her way.

She crossed the yard to the house, more bewildered than before. She felt Graham was friendly towards her but she wasn't certain of his motives. His bantering confused her and she wondered if he wasn't deliberately playing a role to do just that.

She went to her room, and after drawing the crimson drapes and switching on the chandelier, the faulty light of which always bothered her, she set about changing her clothes and getting ready for dinner. Her eyes fell on the little Highland lassie doll which Donald had given her and which she had left on the dresser top. Her eyes moistened as she picked it up and looked at the bright kilted figure for a long moment. It brought her some peace of mind. She felt it was proof of Donald's love and consideration, and as she replaced it on the dresser she was convinced that he could not be a murderer.

Anna said very little at dinner and addressed most of her remarks to Aunt

Caroline, who presided over the table in one of her alert, garrulous moods. And Austin was also in an expansive mood. He lingered at the table, over his coffee and cigar, long after Anna had excused herself, leaving Laura and Aunt Caroline as his audience.

He was talking mostly for Laura's benefit. "Before the causeway was built across the Strait of Canso," he said, "Cape Breton was an island connected to the mainland of Nova Scotia by ferry service."

"Aye," Aunt Caroline agreed. "And when the storms came in the old days, you had to wait. Sometimes it was twenty-four hours between ferry crossings. I can remember making the trip in winter with the snow coming down in a blizzard and the water so rough it washed over the bow!"

"Aunt Caroline can remember the very early days," Austin told Laura, his cigar held in a pudgy hand. "Of course that was long before my time."

"The lakes and rivers here have the best salmon and trout," Aunt Caroline told her. "My man always said Cape Breton offered the best fishing in the New World."

"Doesn't smoked salmon originate here?" Laura asked, eager to make conversation and take her mind off waiting for Donald.

The others laughed at this, and it was Austin who answered her.

"If you're talking about the unsalted variety of smoked salmon, so popular in the States, you won't find it here," he assured her. "Smoked salmon is unknown in Nova Scotia, although I know they call it after this province."

Laura expressed surprise. "That's a discovery."

"You're not alone in making the mistake," Aunt Caroline told her. "We have to tell folk that again and again."

"We do have plenty of lobster, sole, swordfish and salmon in its natural state," Austin Cameron went on. "And I think we know how to cook them to best advantage."

"It is the Highland Games you'll enjoy," the old woman told her, changing the subject. "We have had many champions in this district."

Austin sat back in his chair. "Graham is one of the best of the solo pipers. It takes a great gift to play the bagpipes as a solo instrument and get the right music out of it. It fair scrapes the soul when you listen to a true piper!"

"Aye," Aunt Caroline was quick to agree. "Graham has taken many a first prize for his piping. And one year he won in the caber tossing."

"True, he did," Austin agreed. "I remember him coming to the stand to get his prize, his lass with him. He was properly proud and it was Fiona Sutherland he was seeing regularly at the time."

As he spoke he seemed suddenly to be aware that he had chanced to hit on a forbidden subject. He at once glanced at Aunt Caroline uneasily, and she offered him a reproving look in return.

"That was years ago," the old woman said. "He was just a youngster. Things have changed a good deal since."

"Aye." Austin Cameron's fat face was grave. "A good deal." Then he turned to Laura and asked, "How were Frank and June when you called today? Does she feel any better?"

"It's hard for me to tell," Laura said awkwardly, her mind still on the fact that Graham and the slain Fiona had once kept company. She recalled how bitter the estate manager had been in his comments about the girl, and saw that he might have had as much, or even more, motive for killing her than Donald. It must have been several years later that Donald had been involved with the girl. Then, with a major effort, she brought her mind back to the question Austin had put to her and added, "She was sitting up in bed and Frank seemed to think she was fairly well. She looks very thin and doesn't seem too strong."

"She'll not see the autumn leaves fall," Aunt Caroline said sagely. "You mark my words. She'll go with the end of summer."

Austin Cameron frowned. "I understand the doctors have only given her a few months more at most. It's very hard on Frank."

"I can see that," she said.

"Well, the Lord's will," Aunt Caroline said, struggling up from her chair and leaning heavily on the silver-headed cane, her thin face showing resignation. "We must leave when we are called and I have been long ready to go."

Austin made a pretense of boisterous laughter as he assisted her toward the door. "You'll probably outlive the lot of us," was his optimistic prediction. To Laura, who was walking along with them, he said, "Donald is certainly late. You say he's having dinner in town with one of the cattle merchants?"

"Yes," Laura said. "He should be here anytime now."

She was nervous and decided to go on to her room to wait. Seated in an easy chair, she tried to read but her mind kept wandering from the printed pages of the book. Yet, it gave her time to think her position out and decide the stand she would take. Later, when she heard her husband's familiar step in the hall, she was able to put the book aside and rise with her mind made up as to just what she was going to do.

He looked boyishly happy when he came into the room. He took her in his arms and said, "I believe you've brought me good luck. I put over a wonderful deal today."

"I'm so glad." She smiled, trying to match his mood.

"How did your day go?"

"It was a busy one," she said lamely.

He stared at her, and she was certain he saw in her face what she had been anxious to conceal. It would not be hard for him to guess, knowing how June felt about him and that she had been there for a visit. Yet he had willingly allowed her to go.

Donald took her hand and led her over to the bed to sit on its edge beside him. Very casually he said, "Tell me about it."

Somehow she did. Her eyes averted from his as she faltered over the bare details. She did not elaborate, or even mention, the conversation that had taken place later between her and Anna. Or the meeting in the stable with Graham. When she finished they sat in silence for a moment. She still avoided looking at him directly.

At length he sighed. "So it's over. You know at last."

She turned to stare at him. "Did you think you'd always be able to keep it from me?"

"I had some kind of crazy idea like that," he admitted. "Gradually I've realized it wasn't practical. I knew there was a risk of your hearing when I let you visit Frank's place today. June is a little mad on the subject."

"I know," she said. "It would have been easier if I had heard it from you. Even as late as when I asked you why you wouldn't take me to Frank's yourself."

He looked down. "I made a mistake," he confessed. "I handled it badly. I suppose you're finding it difficult to forgive me."

She touched a hand to his arm. "I'm trying hard to understand," she said. "And I think I do. All along I've felt there was some curtain between us. This has been it."

He turned to her, a mask of grim weariness showing on his face. "Thank you, Laura," he said quietly, as he took her in his arms.

This day, that had seemed destined to stand out forever in her memory as one of the truly dark spots in her life, was suddenly changed. In the warmth of her husband's embrace she felt a happiness as ecstatic as any she had known. It was all the more sweet because of its unexpectedness. She had managed to suppress her fear and doubt, and he had convinced her with his sincerity that anything he had tried to conceal had been an attempt to act in her best interest.

She felt that with this unhappy secret out in the open and shared by them, they could now move on to a more satisfactory married life. Yet there was still the memory of the attack on her about which she had not told him. And since she had remained silent so long, she did not feel like burdening him with a new worry at this moment when they were both reaching out for a fresh beginning.

There could no longer be any question that Anna was still in love with Donald. The girl had not said so outright, but her manner had left no doubt of it. Laura had been tempted to challenge her and then changed her mind. It was bad enough to have it a cause for silent hostility between them without an open quarrel. Anna would continue to love Donald and hope to win him for herself. She would stand by waiting for her to make a false move.

So, even during this happy interlude in her husband's arms, she was aware of the difficulties they would still face. It would take more patience and understanding on her part and more frankness from him, if they were going to manage. And she was especially suspicious of John Graham and the part he might be playing; John Graham who might well have Cameron blood in his veins and who had as much love for the estate as Donald; who was almost a double for her husband and who had been one of Fiona's many men friends.

Later she turned to her husband in the darkness and asked, "How long has John Graham managed the estate?"

"He came as assistant to Noel McCallum about five years ago," Donald said. "When McCallum died he took over. He's done a good job. Why do you ask?"

"It just came to me," she said, pausing a moment. "Are you sure you can trust him?"

"I'd stake my life on him," her husband assured her. "Why all these questions about Graham?"

"No reason," she said, too casually. She reached out to find her husband's hand on the coverlet and took it in hers. "I know he's important in the running of things here. I'm glad you do put so much trust in him."

She worried, however, because she knew her words were the opposite of what she was thinking. And she realized that the curtain of suspicion was still there. The shadow of an unknown murderer still threatened their happiness.

CHAPTER SEVEN

Sunday was the third day of warm sunshine in a row. As soon as they had finished with breakfast, Donald insisted that she make preparations for their drive to the Cabot Trail. He seemed in such good spirits and so enthusiastic about going that she felt it would be wrong to discourage him, although she still had a sense of emotional exhaustion from her ordeal of the previous day.

"We'll need a lunch," he told her. "You get something together quickly while I check the car and have a chat with Graham before we leave." He started for the door and then turned to add, "By the way, we won't be coming back here for the evening meal. The MacGregors have asked us to go there when we return and dine with them. You haven't met them yet."

"But I'll not be dressed for going out to dinner," she said. "My hair will probably be a sight by evening and I'll likely look awful after a day of picnicking."

"Don't worry about it," he said with a

smile. "Glenna and David are two of my oldest friends and they don't stand on ceremony."

She sighed and smiled wistfully. He was like a child when he had these moments of enthusiasm. "Do we really have to go there tonight?"

He looked upset. "I promised Glenna when I saw her in town last night."

"Oh?"

"I suppose I could phone them before we leave. Although it's hard to say if I could catch them. They may be off somewhere themselves on a day like this."

"I see," she said.

"Suppose we just leave it," he suggested. "If we're very late or you do feel badly, we can always cancel out at the last minute. They're not the sort to mind."

"I wouldn't do a thing like that," she protested. But he hadn't waited to hear her. He was already on his way through the door.

She had never met the MacGregors and not even given them much thought until yesterday when June Cameron had referred to them so caustically and blamed Glenna MacGregor for causing the break between Donald and Fiona Sutherland. From June's description, Glenna must be a rather undesirable young woman with a crush on Donald and willing to cheat on her husband to hold his attentions. Laura did not put too much stock in June's picture of the woman. It seemed she had distorted the truth about Fiona in painting her in glowing colors and it was quite possible that she had painted Glenna Mac-Gregor much more blackly than was just.

Still, there might be some truth in the sick woman's account of things. And just now Donald had admitted to seeing and talking with Glenna the previous night. Had she been the cattle merchant his dinner appointment had been with? Or had he just happened to meet her accidentally? He had certainly been late enough in returning, and June's version of his relationship with Glenna raised a disturbing question.

Laura busied herself at the kitchen table making sandwiches and preparing a thermos of coffee, which she packed in a small basket. She was finishing this task when Mrs. Basset entered the room. She was carrying an armful of clothes from the bedrooms upstairs on her way to the washer, which was in a large anteroom off the kitchen.

The housekeeper paused to say, "You

158

should have told me you wanted a lunch. I'd have had it ready for you."

Laura smiled. "I wasn't sure we'd be needing it. In any case, you have plenty of work to do."

"You don't cause any. It's been a grand help the way you do your room. Are you going up to the park?"

"Yes. I'm looking forward to it."

"You'll have it to yourself," Mrs. Basset predicted. "The tourists haven't come yet. It's a good day for it."

It turned out to be a delightful day for the drive to the Highland National Park. The air was warm and there was hardly any traffic. Donald described the country as they drove along and he told her how it had gotten its name from John Cabot's landing near Cape North in 1497. They passed the little town of Dunwood where Austin was a professor at the Gaelic College and went on to the more mountainous and rugged sections of the trail.

Every once in a while the road would suddenly dip toward the ocean and they would find themselves close to the shore. Here they saw swaybacked fishermen's cottages and old-timers mending their nets. Donald pointed out the lobster pots and killocks, the stone-weighed wooden anchors that he explained were typical of the island.

Then as the road rose again, they continued their journey along the coast in the late, sun-drenched morning. Laura was vaguely reminded of the cliff roads on the shores of the Mediterranean. The intense luminosity of the air, combined with the red rocks, the blue sea and the pine trees, were reminiscent of Cezanne country.

She told Donald her impressions. "It reminds me of Europe."

"I think it has a lot of faces," he agreed. "Sometimes I think of Southern Europe, and then the light changes and the landscape suddenly has a Nordic look. It's quiet and mystic and Scandinavian."

Settling back in her seat, Laura watched the changing scene in silence for a time and saw that what he had said was true. It was a spectacular and majestic country; no wonder the first Scots who had landed here saw in it a good deal of their own beloved Highlands.

As they drove on, she asked, "What sort of people are the MacGregors?"

He glanced from the wheel with a smile. "You're not still worrying."

"No. But I've been wondering about them since we're soon going to meet."

He kept his eyes on the road as they were on a section with an abrupt drop on their right. "Glenna is a little older than you," he said. "She's a redhead and pretty. David is about fifteen years older. He's a good solid person but a poor earner, so she works."

"I hadn't heard that before," Laura said.

"I probably took it for granted you knew. I forget this is not your home area. She's worked as long as they've been here. She looks after the books and office for a doctor who is located in the same building where Frank has his law office."

"I see," she said. And guessed that would be the answer to June Cameron knowing so much about Glenna MacGregor. Her husband probably saw her every day.

"Glenna is jolly, a good sport," Donald enthused. "David is inclined to drink too much at times, but otherwise he's a fine fellow."

Laura decided that this fitted in well with the account June had given her. And again she wondered how much else of her story might be true. She tried to sound casual as she inquired, "Do they get on well together?"

"As well as most couples, I guess," he said evasively. "We'll stop at Ingonish for our lunch and then go on to the northern tip of the island."

They stopped at a campsite and spread their lunch on a log table. They were the only ones there and enjoyed a leisurely snack and conversation. She had never known Donald to be quite so talkative and enthused. He seemed almost too much on edge, but she put it down to his relief in at last knowing that he no longer had any need to conceal the shadow in his past, or worry about it. In contrast to his usual quiet, dour personality, he was showing this outgoing side of his character.

Lunch over with, they drove on, taking an improved road past Sugar Loaf Mountain out to the Bay St. Lawrence. They went on to nearby Money Point where the first Atlantic Cable was landed in 1867. He made all these facts of history vivid to her by linking them with personal reminiscences of his family. His great-grandfather had been at this very spot when the cable had been completed. He parked the car on a turnout overlooking a cliff and they got out for a stroll.

A gull swooped close and uttered a weird cry and then drifted gracefully off toward the ocean. Laura smiled at her husband. "Mrs. Basset said we wouldn't meet many people at this time of year. She was right. We have this place all to ourselves."

He nodded. "Unspoiled country! There isn't much of it left. And I wouldn't like to say how long we'll be able to hold back the wave of population here."

"At least you don't have to worry about Cameron Castle's grounds being split up into housing developments for rows of matchstick houses for a while."

"Not in our time, I hope," he said grimly.

"I can't imagine this island ever being crowded with people," she said, staring down at the wide beach hundreds of feet below them.

"We get enough here every summer," he said. Then, glancing to the right, he told her, "There's a natural path along the cliff just ahead. I've often walked it. It gives you a much different impression from standing up here. It leads to a ledge with an excellent view of a small cove." He smiled at her. "Are you game to walk it with me?"

She hesitated. "I don't know. These shoes are not the best for it. Is it very dangerous?"

He laughed good-naturedly. "In my book it isn't dangerous at all. I've walked along there dozens of times. It won't seem like I've made the trip unless I do walk it."

She was going to suggest he go alone but knew that would spoil much of the fun for him. It was plain he wanted to introduce her to this special attraction of the cliffs.

"If you're so familiar with it I suppose it can't really be dangerous," she said.

"Don't worry about it," he told her, his face all smiles, "I'll lead the way and you can hold onto my hand."

"I'm not afraid of high places," she said as they strolled near the edge of the extremely high cliff. She saw the place where the narrow path on its face began. The face of the cliff was almost sheer rock with here and there a few bushes, a lone stunted tree jutting out, or a rough protuberance of rock. Below, there was an almost direct drop to a jagged line of boulders fringing the beach. It was a sight to bring abject fear to anyone sensitive to heights.

Donald's hand was on her arm. "You're sure you're not afraid."

She smiled up at him. "I won't say it isn't scary. But I have a good head, and I'll have you to depend on."

He squeezed her arm. "That's the spirit," he said.

He went ahead and was extremely cautious in getting down to the level of the path which was really nothing more than a bare foot of fairly even ledge jutting out from the cliff face. It was reached by widely spaced steps worn over the years by thrill seekers making their way to the ledge. It struck her that it might be more tricky finding their way back up than descending. He turned to assist her and once her heel caught in a crevice and she almost stumbled.

"Careful of that," he warned with a small laugh. "We haven't much margin for error down here."

Even though heights didn't make her dizzy she refrained from looking down as they made their way along the uneven, narrow ledge. She preferred to keep her eyes on level with the ocean where a freighter sluggishly crawled along the horizon, black smoke trailing after its funnels.

Her husband kept his hand in hers and moved along ahead, not more than a step at a time. "In a moment we'll have the view of the inlet," he promised. "This takes me back to my college days."

"Has it been long since you were up here?"

He nodded. "Yes. The last time Fiona

and I —" He halted awkwardly and then continued, saying, "When we were up here it was in the late fall and almost dusk before we managed to get back up to the road."

Pretending to ignore the slip he'd made and his embarrassment, she smiled and said, "That would make it even more exciting."

"Almost too exciting," he said grimly. "Here we are." The ledge widened and they were able to stand side by side reasonably relaxed and study the magnificent view of beach and ocean spread before them. Privately Laura decided it wasn't a much better vantage place than the spot where they had parked the car. But all men were youngsters at heart and she had been willing to indulge Donald in this boyish enthusiasm.

He smiled at her. "Well, we made it."

Her eyes were bright. "I'll cheer when we're back in the car."

"No worry," he assured her. "We'll enjoy this for another few minutes and then begin the return journey."

She had the feeling that a certain tautness had come into his manner; an underlying nervousness that he was anxious not to betray. She began to worry that he might be shaky about starting the return trip which she'd known from the first would be more difficult.

"Well, no use delaying," he said almost abruptly, and edged by her so he could take her right hand and lead the way back.

Laura began to feel nervous and uncertain. It reflected in her movement along the ledge. Twice she stumbled and each time Donald rebuked her in an almost irritable tone. She began to tremble a little and prayed that they would soon be safely back on the road. She decided she would never take a similar chance again. It was much too risky for the pleasure involved. They had deliberately placed both their lives in danger for his passing whim.

Now they were back at the spot where they must carefully climb up the worn steps to the edge of the cliff. Donald went ahead and reached down to help her to the first step. She was never certain of what happened next.

She heard his frightened cry. "Look out!" Then her hand slipped from his and she toppled back. A scream issued from her lips as a vision of the deadly drop to the jagged rocks below filled her mind. She fell only about ten feet before she struck one of the stunted trees that dotted the cliff face. With a presence of mind made keener by the knowledge that this offered her her one chance to live, she clutched the rough branches of the small evergreen and prayed that it would hold her weight.

She was almost immediately aware of her husband shouting to her. She had no idea what his words were but could tell they were meant as encouragement. Then she thought she heard other voices, strange male voices in an excited clamor, but she was too terror-stricken and weak to pay much attention to them. Her hands were cut and scratched and her arms ached. She dared not try to get a better hold on the small tree, fearing that the slightest movement might send her down the hundreds of feet below.

She clung on, realizing that her strength was ebbing and that it was now only a matter of minutes, perhaps seconds, before she would faint, let go her precarious hold and fall to her death. She fought to remain conscious and she concentrated so deeply that at first she was unaware of the urgent cries now coming to her from above.

Only when she saw the shadow of a man's feet above her did she realize someone was on his way to her rescue. Hope surged in her weakly. Then the figure was close to her and strong hands grasped her body so that she was able to relax and let the darkness take over.

A stranger was bending over her when she opened her eyes. She stared at him stupidly, deciding that he had a pleasant young face although it was now frowned with concern. He was talking to her, almost angrily it seemed. There was another young man, wearing a uniform with a broad khaki hat, standing next to him. But she saw no sign of her husband.

Her first word was a weak, "Donald!"

He came into view at once, kneeling at her side. "It's all right, Laura," he assured her. "Everything is all right."

The Mounted Policeman without the hat gave her husband an angry glance. "It wouldn't have been if we hadn't come along when we did. You'd both likely be down there on the rocks by now."

Gradually she came back to full consciousness and was able to sit up and then stand weakly, leaning against her husband for support. She began to piece together what had happened in the moments following the accident. By a stroke of good fortune a highway patrol car with two Mounted Policemen had pulled up as she and Donald had been making their way back along the ledge.

They had been there, watching from above, when she'd fallen. One of them had quickly gotten a tow rope from the car, tied one end of it around his waist and had his companion and Donald lower him down to her. Only the fact that the rope was available and that the Mounties had been trained for this kind of quick action in the face of disaster had saved her.

But now the Mounted Policeman was angry. The immediate danger was over and he lost no time in condemning Donald. "You must have been out of your mind to take your wife down there. Those ledges are far too risky. We have trouble keeping teenagers off them, but you're a grown man!"

"I'm sorry," her husband apologized.

"You know what would have happened if we hadn't been here," the young Mountie raged on. "I should charge you with recklessness and put you before a judge."

Laura felt she should come to Donald's aid. "We had no idea anything like that would happen," she said. "My husband had been down there many times before."

The young policemen exchanged disgusted looks. "You may be able to forgive him this foolishness, but I can't. If that rope had snapped, you and I would both be dead right now."

She bowed her head. "I know," she said in a low voice. "And we are thankful for what you did."

"That would hardly have satisfied my widow," the young Mountie said with irony. "I can do without thanks. I only ask for common sense."

Donald protested. "I've admitted I was wrong, officer. What more do you want?"

The Mountie hesitated. "Is your wife well enough to drive now?"

Laura spoke up quickly. "I feel perfectly all right." This was a gross exaggeration. She was aching from head to foot; her dress was torn in several places, her hands were cut, and along her left cheek was a stinging scratch. But she wanted to placate the irate young Mountie.

The Mountie looked doubtful. "I'll see you both in your car and on your way before I leave." Still frowning at Donald he asked, "Isn't your name Cameron?"

"Yes. Donald Cameron. We were just about to start home."

"I've seen you before," the Mountie recalled. "At the time of the Sutherland murder."

Donald went chalk white. "I don't rcmember you."

"Not likely you would," the Mountie said. "I had no direct contact with you. I was a new man here then." His glance moved to Laura. "And you say this is your wife?" The emphasis was on the word "say."

Laura frowned. "I am his wife."

"Your husband is a very careless man, Mrs. Cameron," the Mountie declared, his face set grimly. "If I were you, I'd be extremely cautious."

"Thank you," she said. "It's good advice. We're not apt to try mountain climbing soon again."

"I was speaking in a general way, Mrs. Cameron," the policeman said and tipped the broad brim of his khaki hat.

The policemen stood by in solemn silence while Donald walked with her to the car and helped her in. They were still watching when they drove away. He sat at the wheel for a full five minutes before he said anything. Then he startled her by muttering an oath.

"You shouldn't feel that way," she said. "We ought to be thankful to them."

"You heard the way he spoke to me," her husband raged. "He acted as if I were a criminal."

Laura felt too weak and ill to argue.

Even worse, she was beginning to wonder if what had happened had really been an accident. Was it possible that her husband had deliberately set out to murder her this way? That he had faked his stumble and callously let her hand slip out of his, expecting her to drop straight down those hundreds of feet?

He had been balked by two unexpected circumstances, if that had been his plan. He had not counted on the tree breaking her fall and he had not known of the arrival of the Mounted Police car with the two officers. She glanced furtively at him as he hunched over the wheel, driving recklessly, filled with anger for the men who had rescued her. It was terrifying. He was behaving like some sort of mental case. She had noted the reluctance of the officers in allowing them to leave, and she was certain that they believed her husband had meant to murder her.

All the horror was flooding back again. The brief interval of happiness she had known was gone; irretrievably lost this time, she feared. In her present mood she felt she could never trust him again. She had read the suspicion and scorn in the mounted policeman's face and had seen all her husband's bravado crumple before it.

Now he was ranting about the way he had been treated instead of being grateful for her rescue.

Perhaps he sensed her thoughts because he began to drive at a more normal rate and his face lost some of its pallor. He glanced at her and said, "I realize the main thing is that you were saved."

"It was very close," she reminded him in a low voice.

"I know." His eyes were fixed on the road. "I'll never forgive myself for stumbling and allowing you to slip away."

"Accidents will happen," she said in a listless voice that reflected the despair she felt.

"I'll never be able to explain it to you," he said. "I can't explain it to myself."

"Is there any point in going over it again and again?" she asked him. "It only makes you feel worse without doing any good."

"I failed you," he said simply.

"You stumbled," she corrected him, but they were words without conviction. She could only try to save face by saying them. She could bring no peace to her troubled mind with the thin excuse.

They drove on toward home. And as if touched by the terror and unhappiness she felt, the sun retreated behind clouds.

The late afternoon became as dark and ominous as her own thoughts. Before they reached the outskirts of the college town of Dunwood, rain started to spatter the car's windshield and Donald turned on the wipers.

For a long distance he sat at the wheel without saying anything to her. She was bewildered and shocked at his behavior. It was almost as if he had experienced a massive frustration and was now thinking his way out of it. He seemed unmindful of her and uncaring of her condition.

She knew they were only twenty miles from home now and she was concerned about their proposed dinner engagement with the MacGregors. He seemed to have completely forgotten about it. At least, he hadn't discussed it, but then he had talked so little on the return drive.

Sitting forward, she told him, "I can't think of going to the MacGregors the way I am now."

His face was grimly set. "I know that."

"We should give them some notice," she insisted. "I don't want to cause them any trouble. There's a phone booth by the roadside just ahead. Why not make a call from there and let them know we won't be coming."

"We don't have to do that," he said, showing no sign of slowing the car.

Laura felt her anger rise. "I want you to do it!" she said sharply.

It seemed to break through his aloof, sullen mood. He gave her a quick glance of surprise. "All right, if you insist," he said.

"I do insist," she told him firmly.

In answer he braked the car to a screeching halt on the wet road, a few hundred feet beyond the public phone box. With another muttered oath he backed the car up in the near darkness until they were alongside the booth. He got out quickly and went over to it.

Watching him, Laura had a sudden flash of sympathy for his plight. Perhaps she was again condemning him too hastily. No doubt he was filled with guilt and self-hatred for having failed her so miserably. Added to that had been the stern attitude of the police and their bringing up the murder case. There were reasons for his being so upset, and his extraordinary behavior didn't have to be taken as a sign of guilt.

In fact, if he had intended to stage an accident and kill her, it wasn't likely he would have arranged a dinner party for them that very evening at the MacGregors.

This thought strengthened her conviction that she might be judging him too harshly, and all at once she wanted to make amends. She had a sudden idea. It might be gracious for her to speak with Glenna MacGregor personally and apologize for not being able to come. She would have to hurry before he made the call and hung up. She quickly opened the car door and followed him over to the phone booth.

The door was only partly closed as she hurried up to it. Pulling it open, she suggested, "Let me talk to Glenna myself. I think it would be nice for me to make my own apologies."

"It isn't necessary."

"I'd rather," she insisted.

He fumbled at the pay phone again with some change. "I haven't been able to get them," he said.

"They must be home if they're expecting us to dinner," she said, standing partly inside the booth to shelter herself from the light rainfall.

"I can't help it," he said with some annoyance. "I've tried their number but I can't get any answer."

"Try again," she suggested.

He did. She could hear the phone at the other end of the line ringing over and over.

At last he slammed the receiver down in disgust. "This is a travesty," he snapped. "They aren't home and that's all there is to it."

"Don't you think it strange?" she asked, studying his angry face.

"Everything is strange to you, it seems," he said with biting sarcasm. "I can't pretend to follow your thinking. And I don't intend to stand here arguing in the rain."

They went back to the car. Dusk had settled in and he switched on the headlights as they drove on without a word passing between them. Laura sat with closed eyes, trying to control her frantic thoughts. His inability to contact the MacGregors by phone had again brought all her fears clamoring to the forefront of her mind.

Surely it meant that the MacGregors had not been expecting them; that he had made up the story. It fitted in with the planned accident. He had not worried about cancelling the dinner engagement before they left because it had never been made in the first place. He had never intended she should return alive. The realization left her so miserable she was unable to restrain a faint moan escaping from her lips.

"What's the matter?" he asked.

"Nothing. It's just that I'm feeling so thoroughly miserable," she said.

"We'll be home in a few minutes," he told her, and now he sounded more like his normal self and actually worried about her. "I'm sorry it turned out so badly."

She sat with closed eyes and attempted no reply. Once again she was faced with a situation in which she must decide what her husband's actions had meant. He could be either a completely innocent and emotionally mixed-up individual or he could be the cunning murderer many people still thought him. At the moment she was too exhausted to cope with the choice she must make.

At last they reached the great stone house which looked more forbidding than ever before. The rain had begun in earnest and so he let her out at the front entrance.

"Do you need any help getting in?" he asked.

She shook her head. "I'll be all right." Closing the car door, she hurried up the broad stone steps, leaving him to take the car around to the garage in the rear.

There was no one in the dimly lighted hallway when she entered. The first thing her eyes fastened on was the hall phone on its table near the big grandfather's clock.

At once she was struck by an impulse to try a call to the MacGregors and satisfy her curiosity before her husband returned from putting the car away for the night.

Knowing she was strictly limited in time, she stepped quickly to the phone table and picked up the directory with hands already trembling a little. A frantic search of the local pages produced the number and she dialed it. Her heart was beating faster and she cast an apprehensive glance toward the front door fearing Donald might return and find her making the call.

The phone rang over and over. Just when she felt she must put the receiver down a male voice answered. In a faltering voice she asked, "May I speak with Mrs. Glenna MacGregor?"

The man at the other end of the line sounded sleepy and annoyed. "My wife is away for the weekend," he said.

"Thank you," Laura said and slowly returned the phone to its cradle. She stood there, her face drained of color, certain now that her husband's talk of having dinner with the MacGregors had all been part of his parcel of lies.

CHAPTER EIGHT

The days that followed were almost unendurable. Laura was tormented by the realization that her husband could be a murderer who had tried to make her his second victim. The doubt that lingered in her mind kept her from outright despair. She remained on at Cameron Castle hoping that something would happen to erase her fears and restore her belief in Donald. The thought of facing life with the knowledge that he was truly a murderer was unbearable. She had married Donald for love and her love for him was still very real.

Anna's bitter words still haunted her. The girl had made it plain that she did not doubt Donald. That she loved him no matter what. But Laura, as his wife, was in a somewhat different position. If there should be any truth in the story of his guilt, he had deliberately married her with this shadow over his head. He had linked her to the horror without regard for her. She could not see such heartlessness in him, so she clung to a fragile belief in his innocence.

The incident on the cliffs had shaken her, and the attitude of the police had made their suspicions concerning her husband all too clear. But they could be as prejudiced and wrong as anyone else. She must believe that. She must continue to regard what happened as an accident. Donald had lost his balance and let her go without being able to help himself. He had done everything he could to aid in her rescue. She was sure he would somehow have saved her even if the police hadn't been there. The police had been on the scene, however, so she could never be certain.

Then there had been the secret phone call she'd made to the MacGregors and David MacGregor's puzzling reply that his wife had gone away for the weekend. It indicated that they hadn't been expected as dinner guests at all in spite of her husband's story. This brought up the troublesome question of why Donald had indulged in such an elaborate lie. They had said little at the castle about the accident and none of the others had questioned them about it.

The weather had changed to match her mood. The warm days of sunshine had vanished and now there came a monotonous parade of rainy and foggy days. Mrs. Basset accepted the weather cheerfully and assured Laura it was only a passing phase. It was normal for this season of the year and a necessary prelude to the summer's growth. Laura found it merely depressing and hoped it would end soon.

It also seemed to have its effect on the others in the household. As one drab, dark day followed another, she could see the ancient Aunt Caroline droop noticeably. Melancholy seemed to consume the old woman. She formed a disconcerting habit of parading up to the room near Laura's, where she had the rich oak coffin set out on a tablelike stand, and studying for long periods the ornate casket with its metal handles and rich, white velvet lining.

Laura felt it was bad for Aunt Caroline and tried to ignore her vagaries in this direction. Anna was meticulously polite and nothing more. She now avoided being left alone with Laura, although she would exchange a few words with her when they were with the others. Laura could tell by the way Anna watched Donald across the table, and by the special smiles she reserved for him, that she was still in love with him. John Graham seemed to take it all in with quiet amusement and Laura was certain there were depths to the estate manager no one guessed. Austin Cameron was nearing a publication date for one of his Gaelic manuscripts and was more absorbed in this delving into the past than ever. Most nights found him laboriously working on translations until the small hours.

Laura hoped that the others hadn't noticed the strained relationship between Donald and her, but couldn't be certain about it. Aunt Caroline continued to make her preference of his brother Frank obvious. When he did not visit the castle regularly she always fretted.

It was on a late Friday afternoon, a day of dull skies and intermittent heavy showers, that Aunt Caroline announced, "June is feeling well enough to be alone and Frank is coming to dinner tonight."

She and Laura were seated in easy chairs before the fireplace in the living room. Because of the cool damp day, Mrs. Basset had started a cheerful log fire that provided a pleasant warmth as well as extra light for the darkly shadowed room.

Aunt Caroline studied the multi-colored flames with a faraway expression on her thin, parchment face. "I always feel better after Frank has visited," she said. "What a fine man he has turned out to be."

Laura also felt respect for Frank, if only because of his consideration for his ailing wife. "I like him," she agreed.

The old woman frowned at the blazing logs. "This has not been a happy house, my dear," she said. "It began with murder and violence and the shadow of Sheila MacLeod has been over us for more than a century."

She knew what Aunt Caroline was thinking. The fact that Donald had been questioned in the murder of Fiona Sutherland had badly upset her. And even though the authorities had made no charge against him, she felt that history might have repeated itself. Laura could sympathize with her because of her own dilemma.

"But that's giving way to superstition," she said. "Surely you don't believe in ghosts or the curses they impart."

"In Scotland there used to be a verdict in the courts of 'Not Proven,'" the old woman said absently. Her tone becoming bitter, she added, "Not proven is still the worst of verdicts. The disgrace is always with you. The furtive glances and the whispers behind one's back!"

"You're thinking about Donald, aren't

you?" she asked quietly.

Aunt Caroline continued to stare into the flames. She nodded. "Why did he have to get mixed up with that flighty Fiona? He must have known Anna loved him and was right for him!" Then dismay crossed the ravaged face and she turned to Laura all apologies. "Forgive me for thinking aloud, my dear. Of course your coming made everything right again. And I'm sure you and Donald are going to be happy."

Trying to conceal her chagrin, Laura murmured, "I'd like to think so."

"But of course it's true," the old lady said, sitting up very straight and rapping her cane imperiously on the hardwood floor. "You are the ideal person for Donald."

"Why do you say that?"

"You bring a fresh outlook to this dreary old house and this isolated part of the world. The family needs new blood. When all is said and done, Anna is too much like a Cameron to have made a proper wife for him. It was fortunate he met you."

"Still, I often wonder if he is happy."

Aunt Caroline shrugged. "Cameron men have never been known for their display of feeling. You must try to understand him, girl. He was always dour and reticent as a lad, and I suspect he hasn't changed much. But beneath his coldness there was a warm heart. It was true when he was a lad at my knee and I think it is true now."

"He is a sensitive person of great possibilities," Laura agreed. "But he seems to have changed since we came back here. He spends little time on his music and often he hardly seems to notice me."

Aunt Caroline sighed. "You know what happened here. The ordeal he must have gone through. I think he is still tormented by the memory of it. We can only pray that the shadow will pass; that people will forget and he will be able to hold up his head again."

Laura stared at her with troubled eyes. "Do so many people here still think he killed that girl?"

"In a small village like this, suspicion dies hard," Aunt Caroline said. Then her manner changed. "But we mustn't dwell on such things. Frank is coming and I want dinner to be a special one. I think I'll have you get me a bottle of the Cameron sherry. We'll sip a glass now and have it on the table tonight."

"The Cameron sherry?"

Aunt Caroline's eyes twinkled. "My father had it given him by a Yankee captain of a clipper ship years ago. There were six cases in the beginning, the finest of old sherry. The family dubbed it the Cameron sherry and it has been used sparingly down through the years. There are just a dozen or so bottles left, and they are my personal property."

She was amused by the old lady's account. So few things interested Aunt Caroline that it was pleasing to note her enthusiasm. "It must be very special now with all the aging it has undergone."

"It is," Aunt Caroline promised, and rummaged in the small needlepoint bag which she always carried with her. It held the many pills she took on a regular schedule, along with the other common items she had need for such as a hankie, smelling salts and often some strong licorice cough lozenges that came from England. "Here we are!" she announced triumphantly, producing a worn key. "I keep this sherry in a cabinet at the rear of the wine cellar. It is always locked and this is the key. Fetch me a bottle. Take the stairs from the kitchen. They are the handiest. Mrs. Basset will show you the way."

Laura didn't attempt to put off the errand for she knew Aunt Caroline's child-like ways and was sure she'd be uneasy until the errand was looked after. She went directly to the kitchen where Mrs. Basset was busy at the big iron stove. By the numerous pots boiling on its top she guessed the overworked housekeeper was preparing dinner.

"Aunt Caroline wants me to bring her up a bottle of the Cameron sherry from the cellar," she told Mrs. Basset.

The buxom woman shook her head despairingly. "Why now? I can get it for her later."

Laura smiled. "She's pretty insistent. Tell me the way and I'll get it."

"Very well," Mrs. Basset wiped her hands on her apron and crossed to a shelf. "You'll need this flashlight," she said, coming back with a small silver one. "There's something wrong with the cellar lights. They've been off for the last three days and Graham hasn't gotten around to them yet."

She took the flashlight. "Now which way do I go?"

"These are the stairs closest to it," Mrs. Basset said, for there were several stairways going from various parts of the ground floor to the cellar. And she went over and opened the door leading to the steps. "You go straight down and walk until you come to a passage that goes to the right and left. You turn left. Walk straight ahead again until you come to another passage and turn right. The wine cellar is just down at the end of the corridor and the door is always unlocked. We haven't much down there these days."

Laura smiled and held up the key the old woman had given her. "Aunt Caroline keeps her private stock under lock and key," she said. "She mentioned a cabinet in the rear of the wine cellar."

"A big wooden one," Mrs. Basset nodded. "You can't miss it. It's the only one in there." As Laura started down the stairs, the housekeeper added, "Watch your step and don't take a wrong turning. There is an old well at the end of one of the other corridors and it hasn't even a wooden covering. It's no danger when the lights are working but in the dark it pays to be extra careful."

"I will," Laura promised as she snapped the flashlight on. Already she was well down the narrow, worn steps and the dank air of the basement filled her nostrils, and its cold made her shiver a little. She had little knowledge of the cavernous cellars beneath the old mansion but imagined they spread over a large area. It was a world remote from the warm normalcy of above.

It would have been much different if the lights had been working. She supposed that in old houses like this the wiring gave almost constant trouble. By now she had advanced a distance along the corridor and was surrounded by pitch blackness except for the thin ray of light offered by the small flashlight she held. She kept playing it on both the earthen floor and the damp brick walls, wary of missing a passage and taking the wrong turning.

At last she came to the passage and followed Mrs. Basset's instructions by turning left. The ceiling was lower in this corridor and it seemed damper. She was amazed at the distance she went before she came to the second turning the housekeeper had mentioned. Here the beam of the flashlight on the brick walls showed them to be actually wet and the odor of dampness was stronger than ever. She began to have an eerie feeling that she was separated far from those in the upper level of the house and alone in a dark, subterranean area, where all manner of sinister creatures might lurk.

Once, when investigating an old cellar in a Boston house she had come upon a giant rat. It had scudded past her feet and caused her to retreat screaming. Now memories of the hateful incident crowded in on her as she warily advanced along the uneven earthen floor of the narrowing corridor. Something lightly brushed her face and caused her to start with a small cry. Reaching up she discovered she'd caught a section of a spider's web on her hair. It was thick with dust and she brushed it from her with distaste. She was sorry she hadn't waited for Mrs. Basset to do the errand instead of catering to the ancient Caroline by doing it herself.

Her morale had dropped to a low point when she saw the wooden paneled door of the wine cellar a few feet ahead of her. The door was unlocked and when she opened it she let the beam of the flashlight play on the tall racks built to hold bottles at various levels. Significantly the majority of the shelves were empty. She could see only an occasional bottle here and there, deeply covered with dust as a reminder that they were of some old vintage.

Carefully making her way past the racks, she focused the flashlight on a medium-sized wooden cabinet sitting against the rear wall of the small room. The lock showed that it was the one in which Aunt

Caroline kept her special stock and Laura quickly inserted the key and opened it. The old woman had been right in her count. About fourteen bottles lay on their sides in the miniature wine cellar. She carefully removed one of the long-necked, dusty bottles and then locked the cabinet again.

With a sigh of relief she turned and began the journey back upstairs. The beam of the small flashlight seemed woefully inadequate in the frightening darkness. But she was heartened by the knowledge that her mission was half completed and she would soon be out of the cellars. Retracing her steps along the first of the corridors, she had almost reached the first turning when she heard the footsteps behind her.

They came from the direction of the wine cellar though she knew there had been no one there. Yet now she had clearly heard several shuffling footsteps. At once all her submerged fears came rushing to the surface, and terrified she wheeled around and played the flashlight in the direction in which she thought the footsteps had come. She could see no one!

She looked about her with frightened eyes, and hoping that her senses might have deceived her and that it might be

Mrs. Basset coming in the other direction to find her, she called out, "Anyone there?" Her voice echoed hollowly along the low, silent corridors. There was no answer.

Clutching the bottle in one hand and holding the flashlight high in the other, she began to hurry forward. Just as she reached the first turning place she heard the footsteps close again, they seemed directly behind her. She broke into a run, frantic to escape from the darkness and whatever unknown dangers it might conceal.

She had no idea what made her stumble, but when she did, the wine bottle slipped from her hand and the flashlight as well. Worst of all, the flashlight went out as soon as it hit the ground. She was on her knees in the dark, bewildered and terrified. With a muffled cry she groped frantically for the flashlight without any success. Instead she felt the fragments of the lost wine bottle, and fearful of doing more damage to herself with the broken glass, she struggled to her feet and raced on in the darkness.

From the moment of her stumbling to her decision to push on in the dark corridor had only taken seconds. Not long enough, she hoped, to give her pursuer any great advantage. She bumped against first one wall of the brick passage and then blindly lurched against the one opposite. She was certain the footsteps still sounded behind her and it was only a matter of a few more seconds until unknown hands would grasp her. In her frightened haste she lost all track of where she might be and in which direction she might be headed. A belated realization of the danger she faced in plunging ahead in the darkness brought her to a gasping halt. Fighting for breath, she leaned weakly against a damp brick wall. She dared go no further, no matter what happened.

As she waited, still breathing heavily, the footsteps sounded again. They were not so near this time and more hesitant. As if someone might be carefully stalking her. She peered into the blackness trying vainly to discern some sign of movement.

Then from another direction, to the right and ahead, she heard her name called in a familiar male voice. "Laura, where are you?" the voice repeated.

"Here!" she called back. "I've lost my flashlight. I'm afraid to move!"

"Stay where you are! I'll be with you in a minute!" the voice assured her. Then she recognized it as belonging to Frank. She gave a deep sigh of relief. He must have arrived early and Aunt Caroline had sent him to help her.

A moment later the beam of a flashlight appeared and was shone directly on her. Frank came hurrying up, clearly worried. "What in the world happened?"

"I heard footsteps," she said. "Someone seemed to be following me from the wine cellar. I became frightened and stumbled and lost my flashlight. And Aunt Caroline's bottle of wine."

"She won't be happy about that," Frank said grimly. Taking her arm, he suggested, "Let's go back along your route and see if we can locate the flashlight."

"There's no hope for the wine," she said. "The bottle broke."

As they moved slowly along the corridor Frank said, "We'll not worry about that. Just get another and say nothing to Aunt Caroline." He swung the beam of the flashlight along the floor at intervals.

It was several minutes before they came to the place where she had fallen. Frank picked up the flashlight and tried the switch. "Useless," he said. "You likely broke the bulb when you dropped it." Slipping it into his pocket he used his foot to push the broken pieces of bottle to one side. "Too bad to lose that good stuff."

"I was so terrified," she confessed, feeling a little ashamed of her display of fear now.

"You're sure you heard footsteps? Not some other sound that confused you."

She shook her head. "No, there were footsteps."

"Then there has to be somebody else down here," Frank said, holding the flashlight high, "unless you're being visited by Sheila MacLeod's ghost!"

"Please don't talk about such things," she begged.

They continued on and were going down the short corridor to the wine cellar when the door of the wine cellar banged. The sound came from almost directly in front of them and Frank Cameron halted and glanced at her with a startled look.

Very softly he said, "You were right after all!" And he let go of her arm and moved ahead on his own.

As she watched with growing fear, he edged closer to the door and called out, "I'm armed. Whoever you are, open the door and show yourself."

There was a long, complete silence. Frank had his flashlight beamed on the door and Laura stared at it with wide eyes.

Then with a slight creak the battered door began to edge open until a forlorn and disgruntled Austin Cameron stood revealed in the doorway.

"What are you doing down here?" Frank gasped.

The stout college professor looked dreadfully ashamed. "I came down for a bottle. I was short of my own liquor and thought I'd borrow a bottle here. Then I heard her coming. I didn't want her to see me so I switched off my flashlight and moved behind one of the racks. When she left I followed at what I thought was a safe distance. She must have heard me."

"I did!" she exclaimed. "You terrified me and I fell. Why didn't you show your light or identify yourself?"

Austin Cameron raised a pudgy hand wearily. "I've just explained. I wasn't anxious to have anyone know I was down here."

Frank looked grim. "You might have caused this girl's death with your nonsense. Better get on upstairs."

Austin nodded. As he passed Laura with his borrowed bottle in one hand, he paused to apologize in a miserable tone, "I'm sorry for what happened. I know I behaved stupidly. But the others make so much fuss if I take anything from down here." With a hopeless shrug of his shoulders he moved on using his own flashlight now to guide his way.

Frank turned to her. "I should have warned you before. Austin is the secret drinker of the family. You see, we have more than one skeleton in our closets."

"If only he'd called out or showed his flashlight," she said in despair.

"That would have meant letting you find out about him," Frank said. "And his alcoholic's pride wouldn't allow that. We'd better get that other bottle and rejoin Aunt Caroline before she begins to worry about us."

The incident ended. But Laura could not help reflecting how fortunate it had been for her that Frank had come down to look for her. No one had asked him to do it but it seemed he had become concerned about her being down there in the darkness so long and had initiated the search on his own. Another evidence of his kindness and thoughtfulness. Because of Austin's stupidity she could have raced on in the darkness until she'd reached that open well and gone to her death in its murky depths!

The revelation that Austin was a secret

drinker explained why he spent so much of his time alone in his locked room. She felt badly enough for the stout, kindly man to want to spare him the humiliation he would feel if she told the others of the danger he'd put her in. Frank agreed that silence was the best way to handle it.

When they enjoyed the wine at dinner, Laura wondered what the others would think if they knew the story behind bringing it up for their use. Aunt Caroline grew quite gay as the evening wore on.

"How many weeks before the Highland Festival, Donald?" she asked from her place at the head of the table.

"About seven," he told her. "We'll soon be getting out the notices."

Frank, who was seated at the end of the table opposite Aunt Caroline, looked in Graham's direction with a smile. "How about your piping, Graham? Do you think you can hold your own in the bagpipe competition again this year?"

The estate manager looked smug. "I have no doubts," he said.

Austin spoke up for the first time with attempted enthusiasm. "Spoken like a true Scotchman!" he said.

Laura asked, "Do you get good crowds?"

"The whole countryside," her husband

assured her. "It's usually attended by a couple of thousand people at least. Especially if the weather is fine."

Aunt Caroline smiled proudly. "It is the one time in the year when I feel Cameron Castle has a touch of its old glory. And it's fitting our family should be the one to keep up the tradition."

"Not that we can afford it anymore," Anna said with a wry smile.

Aunt Caroline glared at her. "There are sometimes more important considerations than money."

"The county gives us a grant to help pay the costs," Donald pointed out.

Anna gave him a teasing look. "I say the money would be better spent raising teachers' salaries."

Frank laughed. "Come now," he said. "We must keep up at least a little of the old glory. I'm all for the piping, the gay costumes, the singing and the dancing."

"But we should have a party long before that," Aunt Caroline protested, obviously feeling the effects of the heady wine. "Why can't we have a party here early in June?"

"It's a busy time," Donald reminded her. "It could be no more than a small one."

Aunt Caroline's lined face showed a pleased smile. "I don't care how large it is.

Just so we get some gaiety in this old house." With a nod in Laura's direction, she said, "Let's have the party in Laura's honor!"

This brought approval from all those at the table with the exception of Anna Gordon who merely sat staring at Laura with a meaningful smile. When the first outcry had ended, she suggested, "You'll have to include the MacGregors, Donald. It wouldn't be a party without them."

Donald looked slightly embarrassed and Laura realized that he hadn't mentioned them in any way since that Sunday when they had been supposed to go there for dinner.

She looked Donald's way and said, "Yes, you must invite them. I haven't met them yet, you know."

Anna's smile was malicious as too sweetly she assured her, "You're bound to find Glenna interesting."

And before they left the table, plans were laid for a modest house party on the first Saturday evening in June. Aside from the family and the MacGregors, it was decided that they would have only the half-dozen members of the Highland Festival Committee and their wives as guests.

Aunt Caroline said, "Laura and Anna

and I will plan the party and I promise it will be as fine as any in the old days!" With that the old lady signaled for Austin to pull back her chair and help her up from the table.

They all drifted into the big living room and stood around talking. Aunt Caroline was holding court for Austin and Donald in her chair by the fireplace. Anna and John Graham were in earnest conversation nearby and Laura found herself isolated midway up the room with Frank.

He said, "How do you like the idea of the party?"

She smiled. "I can't see that it will do any harm."

Her brother-in-law nodded agreement. "It might do a great deal of good and dispel some of the gloom in this old place."

"I hope so," she said.

"Of course June will not be able to come," he observed with a sigh. "It's at times like this my wife feels the full burden of being an invalid."

"I can understand," she said sympathetically. "I must visit her soon again."

"I wish you would," Frank said. "She feels very badly about the other time. It would make her certain you weren't holding anything against her."

"But of course I'm not," Laura assured him.

Frank glanced down the room to make sure no one was near enough to overhear them and then, with a worried look in his eyes, he confided to her, "I'd like to warn you about something."

"Oh?"

"Glenna MacGregor," he said the name with some embarrassment. "You know she works in the building where I have my office. I hate to have to tell you this. But Donald has been calling for her after work at least a couple of times a week. I've watched them driving off together."

She felt her cheeks flame. "Donald considers the MacGregors his closest friends," she said, defending her husband.

Frank shook his head. "Not the MacGregors. Glenna! David doesn't count. Take my word for it. It came to mind when they were mentioned for the party tonight. As a friend as well as a member of the family I thought I should warn you."

"You think it might be serious?"

"I'm afraid it has been serious since long before you arrived here." He glanced at his watch. "It's getting late and June will be worried. I really must go."

Frank's warning came as less than a surprise. She knew there was a strong link between her husband and Glenna MacGregor. Yet she had not suspected him of seeing her so frequently, or of even currently carrying on this affair.

To add to the bitterness of the discovery, Donald took her in his arms that night when they were finally alone in their room. He seemed elated over the idea of the party.

"Perhaps it will help," he suggested, looking down at her with a gentle smile. "We're much too solemn in this house. I feel we've drifted apart these past weeks. I don't want that to happen."

"Does that really worry you?" she asked, her voice near breaking.

"More than you can guess," he assured her. "Nothing is more important to me than your love." And he touched his lips to hers.

CHAPTER NINE

With the coming of June the weather did another abrupt about-face. The fine clear days returned and now it was getting pleasantly warm. Yet even on the warmest days there was a cool aliveness in the air that Laura found much different from the humid summer climate of Boston. She was gradually beginning to feel like one of the household and in spite of the unpleasantness she had experienced since coming to Cameron Castle she was again beginning to hope that it might turn out well after all.

Donald had been playing the part of a model husband, and the frightening fall from the cliff seemed to fade into the background along with the other unhappy things that had occurred to mar her peace of mind since her marriage. Frank's suggestion that Donald was paying court to Glenna MacGregor behind her back had renewed her fears and insecurity for a while, but in the light of Donald's attentiveness she began to wonder if his brother hadn't been making too much of a relatively harmless friendship.

Planning for the party had drawn them all surprisingly closer together. She was convinced that Aunt Caroline's idea had been a good one. Aunt Caroline had insisted on taking care of the entertainment herself. She was bringing a quartet who specialized in Scottish ballads to highlight the evening, and arranged with the local Presbyterian minister, who had a rich, baritone voice with a true Scots' ring, to read selections from Robert Burns' poems. All in all, the old lady was thoroughly enjoying herself.

She relegated the planning of the dinner and the cocktail hour, along with the sending of invitations, to Laura and Anna. They settled down to the work together reluctantly, but to the amazement of them both they wound up actually enjoying the cooperation.

One June evening, as they finished a session of last minute details at a table in the sun porch, Anna sat back in her chair with a thin smile.

"This has been fun, hasn't it?" she said.

Laura returned her smile. "Yes. I'll be sorry when the party is over."

Anna stared at her. "If we'd met somewhere else under other conditions, I'm sure we'd have been good friends."

"Aren't we friends now?"

Anna gave her a quizzical glance. "You don't honestly think so?"

She sighed. "I think we've made at least some progress. It's hard to be certain. You Cape Breton Scotch have an unusual temperament. Take Graham as an example. Most of the time he is bitterly sarcastic and taunting when he talks with me. Yet I feel he is basically my friend. That all this brusqueness is a kind of bantering."

Anna said, "We're dour Scots, all of us. Even your husband. You'll have to learn to understand us. Graham is only a little more blunt than we are. But then he may have a reason when he thinks that he, but for a quirk of fate, might have borne the Cameron name. Even have been laird of the castle!"

"You think me a Yankee intruder then. All of you!"

"That was my reaction when we first met," Anna said frankly. "Now I'm beginning to see your qualities and understand why Donald suddenly made up his mind to marry you."

"And I'm sure I understand you better as well."

"I'm a complex person," Anna warned, as she stood up.

Laura said, "At least this has proved we can get along in some things."

Anna nodded. "Aunt Caroline is pretty sharp. I wonder if she didn't plan the party with that in mind." She smiled. "Oh, well, I guess we should be thankful for this small truce. And in a few weeks the Highland Festival will be coming along. I expect we'll be asked to help with that."

"We haven't any choice about being friends. Events are bringing us together."

Anna started across to the door leading into the house, then turned in the doorway to say, "If I were your friend I'd warn you that you have a serious rival for Donald's affections who'll be attending the party."

Laura was also standing now. She said, "Of course you mean Glenna."

The other girl gave her a mocking smile. "I can't call you slow."

"It's not hard to be aware of that hazard," Laura told her. "I've heard about it from too many sources. There have been so many warnings I'm wondering if it hasn't been badly exaggerated."

"Another thing," Anna said. "When Donald is at his most charming it's a good time to watch out. I've noticed he's been especially attentive lately."

"I'll be meeting Glenna Saturday at the party," she said. "It will give me a chance to measure her and decide what kind of a threat she is."

Anna smiled knowingly. "All your worst expectations will be realized," she promised.

It wasn't encouraging information and it left Laura feeling that Saturday night couldn't come too soon. She wanted to meet this other woman face to face. In the meantime, she decided she would like to visit Frank's invalid wife again. June seemed to have a fund of local gossip, and Laura had an idea that she could fill her in on more details about Glenna.

Austin Cameron had the afternoon off from the college and was going to the village to visit another professor. He offered to drop her off at Frank's cottage on the way down, and she spoke to John Graham about coming at four thirty to pick her up and bring her back to the castle. The transportation settled, she changed into a light knit dress and had Mrs. Basset prepare her a gift box of frosted orange cake and some sugar cookies.

Austin was still a little shy about the incident in the cellar. On the drive down, he apologized again. "I certainly didn't intend to upset you as I did," he told her, for what was perhaps the twenty-fifth time.

"I know," she said, turning to look out the window at the rich green of the fields and trees, and trying to hide her smile.

"They make so much fuss about my taking a few drinks," he complained. "I have to practice all sorts of deception. Our greatest poet, Robert Burns, didn't stint on his alcoholic intake and it did his work no harm."

"I don't think you should let it worry you," she said.

Austin looked pleased. "I appreciate that, Laura. You're a fine, understanding lass and worthy of a better man than Donald."

"I'm quite content," she said.

"I know that," he went on hastily, "and I meant no harm. In fact, you've done wonders with him. He's beginning to behave in almost a human manner."

Laura stared at him in surprise. "You don't sound as if you have much regard for Donald."

"He means well," his uncle said gloomily. "But he'll never be the man Frank is."

They had come to the familiar white cottage belonging to Frank and his wife, and she prepared to get out. It was the old story. Everyone in the family preferred Frank to her husband. Everyone, she thought wryly, except Anna and herself.

"Thank you for the drive," she said, getting out of the car.

Austin smiled broadly. "It was a pleasure having your company."

June was expecting her and so the front door had been left open in Frank's absence. She took the gifts Laura had brought, thanking her for them, and then put them on the table beside her bed. The frail woman was sitting up with several pillows for support and now she gave Laura an admiring appraisal.

"You're looking very well," she said. "Cape Breton must be agreeing with you."

"It is in many ways."

"Frank said you seemed reasonably happy in spite of everything," June went on. "And I think you're very wise to accept things you can't change." She hesitated. "I've worried about being the one to tell you about Fiona's murder."

"I'm glad you did now that the initial shock is over," Laura said.

"You had a right to know," June agreed. "I have given it a good deal of thought,"

Laura went on. "I'm sure Frank is right in thinking Donald innocent."

June's pinched features took on a stern look. "I'll never agree. I say he cold-bloodedly murdered Fiona."

Laura asked, "Was she such a nice person? I've heard other opinions."

"And of course you would," the sick woman snapped. "In a small place like this the chief pleasure is using a vicious tongue against those they envy. Fiona had beauty and plenty of money and so she was envied."

"Didn't she have a good many boy friends?"

"And why wouldn't she?" June retorted. "She had all it takes to attract them. And she lacked the heartlessness of Glenna MacGregor." Her eyes gleamed. "I hear she's to be at the party Saturday. I wish I could be there to tell her that I consider her a hussy!"

"I wish you could attend at least," Laura said sincerely. "I'll be meeting this Glenna for the first time."

"She's a bad lot," June said with a curl of her thin lip. "And if I were you I'd be very careful."

"In what way?"

"I'd watch that husband of yours," June

warned her. "He killed to protect himself and Glenna once. Why shouldn't he do it again? He'll be more confident this time."

"You shouldn't say such things! You can't prove them!" Laura warned her.

June lay back against the pillows limply and stared at the ceiling. "You won't believe me, and one day it'll be too late. Everyone knows he married you for your money, and when he gets greedy enough and Glenna nags him on he'll do with you exactly what he did to my poor dear Fiona!"

For want of anything better to say, Laura said in a small voice, "I'm not listening to you."

"Where is your precious husband now?" June asked.

"In Halifax for a few days," she said. "He'll be back before the party on Saturday night."

June smiled sourly. "It's a wonder Glenna hasn't followed him to Halifax. I must ask Frank if she was at the office today."

"I refuse to worry about her," Laura said with a touch of defiance. "If Donald loves me he'll be faithful. If he doesn't, the sooner I discover it the better."

"You'll understand more after you see

them together Saturday night," June promised. "And remember I warned you!"

Laura was glad when John Graham arrived to drive her back to the castle. She bade June a hasty good-bye and hurried out. It struck Laura that June's long illness had soured her nature completely. Her mind was twisted and full of hatred. Because she thought Donald responsible for her friend's murder, she could not say anything too vicious about him, or his friends.

When she got in the car beside John Graham, he gave her an amused glance and observed dryly, "You look as if you've been through a bad session."

"It wasn't a pleasant afternoon," Laura admitted. "That poor woman has been twisted by her illness."

"It's likely," he said, as he started the car. "I don't imagine it's much fun to have been confined to that room for years and know you're going to die soon."

"She really hasn't long to live then?"

He shook his head. "No. She has some form of blood cancer, though none of the family will admit it. I talked to the doctor in the village and he says her time is getting short."

Laura at once felt her sympathy for June

Cameron wipe away any anger the woman had raised in her. She was to be pitied and anything she said should be taken with a grain of salt.

Turning to Graham, Laura said, "You and Fiona went together for a while, didn't you?"

He kept his eyes on the road, but his jaw went hard. "If you know that, why ask me?"

"What kind of person was she?"

"I was in love with her. I'd be no judge."

Laura raised an eyebrow. "It must have upset you when she left you for Donald?"

Graham's expression was grim. "There were a few others before she took your husband under her wing."

"Then she was a flirt!" Laura said triumphantly.

"I didn't say that. You did."

"But that's what you meant."

He turned from the wheel to give her a quick angry glance. "What does it matter? She's dead. Why should you care?"

"I'm trying to convince myself that she made a lot of enemies. That there was more than one man who might have felt like killing her." She paused. "My reason is that so many people still think my husband murdered her."

"Is that important?"

"It is to him. And to me!"

"I'd say the only thing that's important to you is whether you think he murdered her or not!"

His words had a stinging impact on her. She knew that Graham was not one to mince words. It was a trait she admired in him but it caught her without an answer now.

At last she said, "I know what I want to believe."

He looked disgusted. "That's a good female answer. It doesn't say anything."

"You're Donald's friend, aren't you?"

"I'm his estate manager," Graham corrected her. "And I hope to continue in the job unless some stupid female causes trouble between us."

"Now who would want to do that?" she asked innocently.

"If I told you, it would probably only bring on another fit of hysterics," he said, as he brought the station wagon to a halt in front of the main entrance. With a smile he added, "You didn't get much information from me, did you?"

"You Scotch!" she sputtered angrily. "You're all such cold fish! The only match for you is Anna Gordon! I wonder you two don't marry!"

John Graham grinned happily. "The truth is I'm a lot more interested in you. But then, you're not free. At least not yet!"

Laura gave a small outraged gasp and let herself out of the car, almost turning over on a high heel in her haste. She strode up the castle steps with Graham's chuckle in her ears. It had not been one of her good afternoons.

Nor was the evening much better. Aunt Caroline, who was already resting in preparation for the party, went straight up to bed after dinner. Both Graham and Anna were going to the village and Laura was left at the mercy of Austin Cameron. He had returned from his afternoon with his associate somewhat the worse for liquor. Even a heavy dinner hadn't improved his condition much. He insisted on talking to her in Gaelic and then giving long-winded translations of what he had said.

After nearly an hour of this, Laura excused herself and hurried upstairs. The house seemed unusually somber and quiet with the others out and Donald away. She locked the door of her room and settled down to read a book. She continued to read until she heard Anna's car returning and some time later John Graham's station wagon. Glancing at her wristwatch, she was surprised to find it was close to midnight. At once she put the book aside and started to prepare for bed.

At first she thought she was dreaming, but when she sat up in the darkness and heard the voice again, she recognized it as Donald's. He was rattling the door handle and asking to be let in.

"Is that you, Donald?" she called out, suddenly wary, although she knew it was possible he had driven home late.

"Of course," the somewhat muffled reply came. "I'm waiting for you to open this door."

"One minute," she said. Sure now that it was Donald, she swung out of bed, put on her slippers, and hurried across to the door to open it.

When she turned the key and swung the door open, there was no one in sight. She experienced a second wave of fear, and staring out into the dimly lighted corridor, she called his name. "Donald? Are you there?"

There was only silence. Debating whether to shut the door and lock it again, or investigate further, she finally decided to step outside and see if she could see where he had gone. The moment she stepped out into the corridor, rough hands seized her from behind. A hand covered her mouth and prevented her from screaming for help while the other neatly slipped something around her throat and began to tighten it.

She struggled wildly, knowing that her attacker had returned and that around her throat was the same sort of cord used to strangle Fiona. She was unable to free herself from the iron grip of her unseen assailant, and as she began to gag and choke, he removed his hand from her mouth to help subdue her struggling. Laura felt the cord around her throat burn in deeper each moment. There was a ringing in her ears and she knew that she was soon going to die.

At that moment she vaguely heard her name called from a great distance, but she was too far gone to care, and was not capable of making any reply. Then everything exploded into light that quickly became a numbing darkness. She couldn't breathe. Not only did it hurt her, but she was locked in some incredibly small, dark room and there was no air! Her throat throbbed with pain and she beat on the door of the room with her fists, but it didn't do any good. She felt her lungs would burst and she was struggling with her whole body now, more conscious of her plight and her surroundings. With a growing sense of horror she knew she was flat on her back and she was in no room but in some sort of long, flat box. As all became clearer, her terror grew almost unendurable. She began to shout for help and try to claw her way to freedom from this prison. Her fear reached its peak when her frenzied fingers felt the softness about her! She was being smothered in this small, softly lined box! Then it flashed through her blurred mind as if in giant electric letters! She was in Aunt Caroline's coffin!

Her attacker had placed her in the coffin and closed the lid. She heaved her body wildly and used all her strength against the satin lined covering that was confining her to this agonizing death. Her lungs sought air and tears ran down her cheeks as she pounded on the lid, the sound of her beating fists muffled by the mockingly soft satin!

Then it gave way. She was able to raise it and send it clattering to the floor. She sat up in the coffin just long enough to get a good breath, and then in fear and revulsion got out of its loathsome confines. She was still trembling and her head reeled so she could barely make her way across the dark room to the corridor. Once out in the comparative security of its dim light, she leaned weakly against the door frame for a moment.

"Laura!" Her name was being called loudly. She straightened up with fear in her eyes, conscious that it could be her attacker playing a game with her again. She marked the distance to the door of her own room and, using the wall for support, managed to make her way down to it.

"Laura!" her name was called again. It was Austin Cameron. He appeared at the end of the hallway, dressing gown over his pajamas and a frightened expression on his face. "I thought you must be awake," he said. "I was in the lower hall and heard what seemed like a struggle going on. I called up but no one answered. Are you all right?"

"I think so," she gasped. "Someone tried to kill me."

"Tried to kill you!" Austin's face wore a ridiculously incredulous expression as he came slowly toward her.

She swallowed and it hurt. She touched her fingers to the burning line that circled her throat. "Afterward he put me in there."

She pointed to the room where the casket was kept.

The professor still looked dazed. "I don't understand. Where is Donald?"

She stared at him. "He's not here! Remember? He's in Halifax!"

"But I saw him just a moment ago," Austin insisted. "I was at the end of the corridor and didn't get a good look at him, but I saw him going down the stairs. He was wearing a dark coat but had no hat."

"You saw Donald on the stairs?"

"Before I started up here. I called to him but he'd vanished somewhere downstairs. I was puzzled at what it all could mean so I came up here."

She shook her head. "No," she said. "No. It couldn't be!"

His eyes opened wide and he spoke hoarsely. "You don't mean Donald was the one who came up here and tried to kill you?"

"It couldn't have been him," she said in what was almost a moan. "You must have made a mistake."

"I don't see how. The light isn't good in the hall, I admit," he said. "But I recognized his face. I know my own nephew when I see him."

"His car," she said. "If he came back, his

car must be parked in the yard."

"I can soon find that out," Austin said, appearing to have recovered somewhat from his shock. "You're in bad shape. I'll get Mrs. Basset to look after you."

"No!" she protested.

"Anna, then."

"No one!"

He looked perplexed. "Well, I can't leave you alone like this. Whoever is responsible may be lurking somewhere in the house."

She fought to regain some control of herself. "I'll lock myself in my room," she said weakly. "You go and check about the car."

He hesitated. "I don't know."

"Please!" she begged. "I must find out."

Austin glanced at the open door of her room. "We'd better check to see if anyone is hiding in there first." He switched on the lights before he very gingerly proceeded to investigate every possible hiding place, including the bathroom and closet. When it was clear there was no one there, he allowed Laura to lock herself in and went to see if Donald's car was anywhere on the grounds.

Waiting for his return was an agony. She helped fill it by applying cold cloths and then a soothing cream to her throat. She knew that Austin was likely right, that he had seen Donald descending the stairs, that he probably was the one who had made this vicious assault on her. But at the same time she was hoping against hope that it wouldn't be proved true. That there would be some clue leading to someone else.

Ten minutes or more passed before the knock came on her door. "It's me," Austin told her. "You can open up safely."

She did and Austin was standing there with a bottle in his hand. "I'd say you need a good stiff shot of whiskey," he told her, making his way to the bathroom and finding two glasses. He poured a little whiskey in one glass for her and a little more than that for himself. Handing her the smaller of the two drinks, he took a big mouthful of his. He coughed and said, "That will help. Go on. Drink up."

Laura hesitated. "First, what about the car?"

He shook his head. "No sign of it."

"Then it couldn't have been Donald you saw."

He looked at her oddly. "I suppose not. I could have made a mistake," he said and took another large swallow from the glass, almost finishing his drink.

Laura took a sip and felt it burn down her throat. She followed it with another and a third. The whiskey at once began to revive her and she felt better.

"Sit down," Austin ordered her. "You don't look too well yet."

She located a chair and sank into it. "This helps," she said, and took another sip of the drink.

The professor was already pouring himself a second generous helping. He said, "I've found it nearly always does."

Laura looked across the room at him. "You don't believe it was Donald, do you?"

"I don't know who it was. You certainly didn't try to murder yourself."

"But you were so sure you saw Donald," she persisted. "We both know he's still in Halifax. You must have made a mistake."

He sighed. "I admit I was at the end of the hall, maybe forty feet from him, and the hall isn't half lighted. But I swear I caught a glimpse of his face or someone who looked a lot like him."

"How about Graham?"

Austin looked startled. He frowned. "You're right. Graham does look a lot like him." Then he shook his head. "But Graham's hair is much lighter than Donald's. I swear I saw dark, curly hair."

"You only had a fleeting glimpse. Can you be so sure?"

He stared into his glass. "Perhaps not," he said, and downed the rest of the amber liquid. He looked at her. "Want any more?"

"No, thanks. I'm perfectly all right now except for my throat. And that will take some time."

The professor said, "What are we going to do?"

She hesitated. "I don't know. I wish Donald was here."

Again he looked at her peculiarly. "We should call the police."

"I can't do that!" she said.

"We should call the police," he went on with the dogged insistence of a man basically weak and unsure of himself. "And we should rouse the others and tell them what has happened."

"What could we accomplish by that?"

Austin was apparently feeling the benefit of his two stiff drinks and seeing himself as the authority in control. His face wore a look of dignity that was almost comic.

"If a murderer is roaming around in the house," he said with undeniable logic. "The others should be warned."

Laura's face was a study in torment.

"Whoever it is has no interest in them," she said dully.

"How can you be sure of that?" he asked. "I might have been attacked when I came up here to rescue you."

He had now arrived at the point where he felt he had been her rescuer. It didn't seem worthwhile arguing this unimportant detail. What she wanted now was time to think it all out and get him back to his bed.

She said, "If you don't get some rest you won't be able to report at the college in the morning."

"Blast the college!" he snorted. "This is more important. Hadn't I better phone the police this minute?"

Laura stood up, and her eyes met his. "You know we dare not do that!"

"Why not?" he asked, perplexed.

"Because you'll have to tell them the story you told me," she said in a low, tense voice. "And once that is done, Donald will be under suspicion again. All the past will count against him. They'll be opening up Fiona's case and charging him with that as well."

Consternation followed perplexity. "What will we do?"

"We'll have to wait until Donald comes back. Get his advice."

Austin swallowed hard. "But if he was the one — and he could be, even if his car isn't here. He could have driven back and made the attack on you and then gone off somewhere. Tomorrow he can return again and claim he's just arrived from Halifax. How are you going to know if he's telling the truth or lying?"

"He's my husband," she said, pretending an assurance she didn't wholly feel for Donald's sake. "I'll believe whatever he says."

"That's noble of you," Austin said with a hint of sarcasm. "But I'm not sure your decision is wise."

"I'm going to be panicked into thinking Donald guilty," she said quietly. "Once I think that, there's nothing left."

He looked unhappy. "I understand," he murmured.

"Now we'd better get back to our beds."

"And leave all these questions unanswered?"

"We can wait a few hours longer," she said. "And not a word to anyone."

He started for the door, and then realizing he was forgetting his bottle, returned for it. As he made his way to the corridor again, he shook his head. "I won't be able to sleep."

She raised her eyebrows meaningfully. "If it offers you any small comfort, I don't expect to be able to either."

CHAPTER TEN

Only when she was in bed, trying to get some rest after Austin had been long gone, did it strike her that he might have been her attacker. The realization filled her with added tension. He had been the only one awakened by the sounds on her floor. He had spoken of seeing Donald leaving but this could easily have been a lie concocted to throw suspicion on her husband since he knew she already was worried about Donald's possible guilt in Fiona Sutherland's murder.

She saw how easy it would have been for him to make the brutal assault on her and then abandon her in the coffin and run for cover thinking she would suffocate in it before she regained consciousness. His return could have been a result of his curiosity as to what had happened. It was easy for him to pretend he'd heard the scuffle and explain that he had come to investigate. It made a perfect alibi. And when he discovered she was still alive, he neatly assumed the role of her rescuer.

231

It was attributing great guile and a generous amount of intelligence to Austin, but one could never be certain of what was behind the facade of a slow-thinking, middle-aged man like the professor. And what would be his motive? Perhaps a plan to eliminate her, and Donald as her murderer. This would pave the way for him to play a bigger part in the affairs of Cameron Castle, now in the clear as far as debts were concerned. It could be mere revenge at his disappointment in Donald marrying her rather than his stepdaughter, Anna. If his mind was twisted enough, there need be no valid reason.

Laura frowned in the darkness. She was allowing her imagination to carry her to fantastic conclusions. When it came right down to it, she couldn't picture the shaken, uncertain Austin as a master criminal. Far more likely, he had told her the truth.

As if to underline this, Austin knocked on her door early the next morning before he left for his classes at the college. Since she was already up and dressed, she came out to chat with him briefly in the hallway.

His face was puffy and his eyes were red, probably as much from helping himself too generously of the whiskey bottle as from lack of sleep. He looked at her worriedly.

"You're certain you're all right?" he asked.

"Yes. Even my throat feels better," she said.

He eyed her closely. "I can still see the red line."

She shrugged. "That's going to be there for a few days."

"I'm still worried about not calling in the police. They should be informed."

"We've gone into that," she told him with a meaningful glance.

He frowned, still hesitating to leave. "I could call the college and beg off this morning," he suggested. "I dislike having you here alone."

"Aunt Caroline will be here, and Mrs. Basset and Graham are within reach. I'll be perfectly safe."

"Donald may return. What are you going to say to him?"

She looked down. "I haven't quite decided. But there will be no trouble. I promise you."

He rubbed his chin and his face was drawn with concern. "I've never been involved in anything like this before. It's most disturbing."

"If I need you I can always phone the college," she told him. "And I will if it comes to that." This promise finally sent Austin on his way.

Laura waited until she saw Anna's car leave as well before going down for breakfast. She had no desire to face the girl in her present frame of mind. Mrs. Basset was her usual cheery self, and by the time Laura left the table to return upstairs, she was feeling somewhat less tense.

Before she went about tidying up her own room she knew she had one other distasteful task to look after. Because she did not want Aunt Caroline uselessly upset it would be necessary to look in on the coffin and straighten away any signs of damage from last night's episode. Laura had always felt a revulsion for the stuffy room with the coffin set out on a table like a fixture in a funeral parlor display room. After being imprisoned in the coffin the night before, she had an even more intense aversion to it, but she felt that going in there now was a duty she could not avoid.

As the rays of the sun did not reach this side of the house until later in the day, the corridor was still in gray shadow as she made her way along it to the small room. Hesitating only slightly, she opened the door and went inside. The drawn blind of the room made it even darker, so she switched on the old-fashioned overhead fixture with its two small bulbs.

In the sickly light she approached the open coffin. Noting that it was at an uneven angle from her exertions to escape from it, she adjusted it to a straight position on the table. Putting aside her feelings of disgust, she made herself pat the fancy tucked satin in place where she had wrinkled it and pulled it out of shape. And as a final touch, she moved the lid from where it had fallen on the floor and smoothed its lining as well. A corner had been scratched on the outside of the lid but she carefully placed it in its former position against the table and hoped that Aunt Caroline would not notice this slight damage.

"What in the world are you up to?"

She wheeled around and saw Donald standing there, looking as handsome as usual in brown tweed sports coat and matching trousers. He looked at her, surprised.

"When did you get back?" she asked.

"Just now. Mrs. Basset said you'd come upstairs and I came to find you. You weren't in our room; then I saw this door open. What are you doing in here?"

Laura gazed very directly at his sensitive face and wondered if his surprise was genuine. Then she said, "That will take some explaining."

He was frowning with distaste. "I thought you felt the same way about this room as I do."

"We'd better go back to our own room," she said. "Something happened here last night. It's time I explained a few things."

He followed her out and along the corridor. "I break records driving back from Halifax to get a good day's work done and I arrive to find you in a crazy mood playing with that coffin," he grumbled.

She closed the door after them as soon as they were in their own room. Then she turned and pointed to the ugly bruise around her throat. "See that," she said quietly.

His eyes opened wide. "What's happened to you?"

He was either an expert actor or he was really startled, she decided. Certainly he displayed all the proper reactions of surprise and concern as she recounted the story of the previous night.

When she finished she said, "Austin was sure it was you he saw on the stairs."

"But I was in a motel in Halifax," he protested. "I left just after dawn this morning."

"Did anyone see you leave?"

He stared at her a moment. "No, I guess not," he said lamely. "I paid for the room when I checked in the previous day. I just packed and left my key on a table. I had breakfast at a diner along the road here."

"So you might have left any time. Even early enough last night to have been here around midnight."

"I could have, but I didn't," he said with some anger. "I hope you believe that."

"I do," she said quietly. "But if Austin told his story to the police, would they be so willing to accept your version of things."

On hearing this Donald looked more than startled. There was actual fear in his face. "Why shouldn't they?" he asked, faltering.

"I'm sure you understand why better than I do," Laura said. "That's why I refused to let Austin get in touch with them."

He sank into a chair across from her, bewilderment glazing his eyes, and said, "How did Austin feel about it?"

"Very upset. He felt the police should be called in."

"He would!" Donald said with a sigh.

She looked at his stricken face. "You have nothing to worry about. I've persuaded him it's best for the family if we keep it to ourselves. Your uncle has a strong sense of family pride."

Donald looked at her in a dazed way. "You sound as if you really think I might be guilty. That I came back here last night and wantonly attacked you."

Laura shrugged. "I'm trying to let you understand what others might think."

He jumped up angrily. "Don't you see what this was? An attempt to throw suspicion on me. Whoever murdered Fiona and left me a prime suspect isn't finished with me yet. Apparently they plan to turn their attentions to you and have me wind up suspected of the murder of my own wife this time! It's a fiendish scheme of the real killer to tie up the other case with a new one so he'll never be suspected."

She smiled wryly. "If all you say is true, neither of us is in an enviable position."

Donald began to pace up and down. "I should never have married you with this hanging over my head. I never should have brought you back here."

"I don't agree with that, but I believe you should have told me the truth and let me come here with open eyes."

He looked at her unhappily. "If I'd done that, you'd never have married me!"

"You don't value my love for you very

much then," she said in a low voice.

He came over to her at once. Taking her hands in his, he drew her up on her feet. "That isn't true," he declared earnestly. "Only the knowledge of your love has sustained me this long."

She found it hard to doubt him at this moment. Looking into his eyes, she said, "It's my love for you that convinces me that you're telling the truth. Otherwise I would be as suspicious as the others."

Donald took her in his arms and kissed her gently. And from her lips he went on to kiss the injured throat and caress it softly with his hand. When he finally let her so, there was a determined expression on his face.

"It's no good," he said. "I'll have to tell the police. Otherwise you'll still be in danger."

"You can't," she said. "Austin will say he saw you on the stairs."

"And I'll say it was someone else," he told her. "Someone he thought was me. He admits he saw the figure from a distance." He paused. With a look of consternation, he asked her, "Why couldn't it have been Graham? Everyone remarks on how much we look alike!"

"I thought of that," she admitted. "I

even mentioned it to Austin."

"What did he say?"

"He claims it couldn't have been Graham. The man was wearing no hat and he saw his hair. It was not sandy like Graham's but dark with a slight curl like yours."

Donald shrugged. "It was only a desperate guess anyway. John Graham is not capable of doing anything like that."

"You can't be sure," she reminded him.

"I have to do something about it," Donald said pacing again.

"I disagree," she said. "Let him make the next move. Whoever he is."

He shook his head. "Too risky!"

"It might turn out as risky for him as for us," she suggested. "Criminals usually run out of luck eventually. I have an idea the tide turned for him last night."

He stopped and studied her with new surprise. "Do you really think that?"

"Yes. Next time he may give himself away."

"You could be right," her husband said thoughtfully. It struck her that his reaction to her words was not exactly what she'd expected.

But a fresh truce was established and it was not altogether an easy one. The following days saw the final preparations for the Saturday party and they were caught up in this excitement once again. Yet there was a new, underlying uneasiness among them. Austin was still privately voicing his concern to her about the police not having been called in and he seemed increasingly nervous, while Donald seemed to have lost interest in the party and to have retired within himself. He spent several afternoons in his study working at his composing and she suspected he was using this sudden enthusiasm for his music as an excuse to be by himself.

His behavior struck her as odd, and all the nagging doubts she had known since coming to Cameron Castle as his bride came back to torment her again. The truth had to be faced. In each instance where she'd been attacked it appeared he had been on the scene. The first time she had been certain she'd caught a glimpse of his face, and the other night Austin had been the witness to his leaving by the main stairway. To add to the mounting proof against him, there was the supposed accident in which he'd let go of her hand and allowed her to fall to almost certain death. Laura made a pretense of enjoying the party preparations but her heart was no longer in them.

On the Saturday morning of the party Aunt Caroline summoned her and Anna into the living room to get their approval of her arrangements for the affair. Leaning on her cane, the old woman said, "You see I have the grand piano and the chairs for the entertainers there by the window. The rest of us will be seated at the rear of the living room. I don't want the chairs formally arranged, just scattered around the walls as they are now so everyone will be at ease."

"I think it's excellent," Anna said enthusiastically. "Don't you agree, Laura?"

She nodded. "Yes. If anyone wants to leave the room it will be easy to do it without disturbing other people."

"Exactly my idea," Aunt Caroline declared. "Not all the guests will want to stay through the entire entertainment. If any of them get bored they can move to one of the other rooms and talk. And we'll be wanting to move back and forth to keep in touch with the kitchen."

The plan was for a midnight buffet after the entertainment and Mrs. Basset had been baking and storing special treats for more than a week. Aunt Caroline turned to the two girls with a satisfied smile.

"I want it to be a good party," she said.

"It could very well be my last one."

Anna impulsively threw an arm around her thin shoulders. "Of course you're talking nonsense. We'll have many more fine times here."

"Perhaps," Aunt Caroline said resignedly. "I hope you will enjoy the party, Laura. It is really for you."

"And I do appreciate all the effort you've put into it," Laura assured her.

Aunt Caroline nodded. "I must check with Mrs. Basset about the wine. We'll need a good stock of it upstairs." With an energy Laura had not noticed in her ever before, Aunt Caroline quickly hobbled off, her cane tapping on the hardwood floor of the corridor.

The two girls were left alone in the living room. Anna looked at Laura with a wise smile. "Is Donald as enthusiastic about tonight as the rest of us?"

"I think so."

Anna arched an eyebrow. "He doesn't strike me as much interested. Perhaps he's worried about you and Glenna meeting."

"Then why did he invite the Mac-Gregors?"

"He could hardly avoid it," the pretty girl said. "David MacGregor is on the committee for the Highland Festival. In small places like this there is only one social group."

Laura knew this was true. On formal occasions such as this party, to omit inviting one of a particular group would be to mark them as someone you felt was undesirable. And she wondered if Donald was really nervous about the approaching meeting between her and Glenna, with whom his name had been so often linked. In the beginning he had at least pretended he wanted her to meet the MacGregors.

As they dressed in their room early on Saturday evening, Donald grumbled, "I don't know why Aunt Caroline insisted on this party. We'll be having the Highland Festival in a few weeks. That should have been enough."

Laura was fastening a single strand of pearls around her neck, the only jewelry she was wearing with her long gray evening gown. "The party is to honor me," she reminded him.

His manner changed. He turned with an understanding smile. "I'd forgotten about that. And you deserve some gaiety after what you've gone through here." He paused to sigh. "I haven't been able to relax since what happened the other night. I've been trying to find some clue to who might have come up here and attacked you, but so far nothing has turned up."

"Remember what I said," she told him. "Whoever it is, his luck will change."

"I'd like to believe that," he said, turning to the mirror again to adjust his tie. "But at the moment I'm still almost inclined to agree with Austin. We should call in the police."

"Not yet," she said, impressed by his earnestness and more than ever certain that he had nothing to do with the attack.

Because all the males participating in the affair were members of one or another of the Cape Breton Highland Regiments it had been Aunt Caroline's idea that they all wear their army dress uniforms. This would make for a colorful gathering in true Scottish tradition. The dress uniform consisted of the usual kilts and their decorations, along with white shirt, dress tie and black jacket. The kilts of the various regiments were in contrasting tartans of red, blue and green.

Laura and Donald went downstairs in time to join Aunt Caroline and the others in the receiving line. The pianist with the singing group was already playing. Aunt Caroline wore a black gown that added to her normally majestic air, and Mrs. Basset had done an excellent job on her upswept hairdo. Anna was pretty in a rose gown, while her stepfather looked overstuffed and unhappy in a uniform which had been tailored for him during his active army days twenty years back, and which he'd worn little since.

The first to arrive was one of the town councillors and his wife. Hardly had they passed along the line when the next guests arrived and so on until nearly everyone was there.

Brisk conversation filled the air and the piano music served as a suitable background, while Mrs. Basset passed among them with trays of drinks. Donald was behaving as if the occasion was more an ordeal than a celebration, and Laura was somewhat on edge because Glenna and David MacGregor had not yet put in an appearance.

The bell rang again and this time the maid showed in a tall, graying man with a very red and rather weak face, along with a much younger woman with an aggressive type of beauty. There was a suspicion of heaviness about the carefully made-up face, and a hardness in the almost too small eyes. But the flaming red hair of the woman in the striking yellow gown gave

Laura the clue that this was Glenna MacGregor. She was about to meet her rival at last.

When Donald introduced them he did manage a smile. It wasn't a convincing one, but Laura decided it was a very good effort. She saw the redhead's eyes take her in quickly with an appraising glance.

"But you're lovely!" Glenna said gushingly, taking her hand and smiling at Donald. "Now I know why you've kept her from us so long!"

"I've been eager to meet you," Laura said evenly, with a polite smile. "So many people have spoken of you."

Glenna lost a bit of her poise. "Really? I had no idea I was such a popular figure!" She turned to Donald again. "Am I such a popular figure, Donald?"

"That's such an old story we take it for granted," he said with gallantry.

David MacGregor took Laura's hand. "Welcome to our Highland wilds," he said with a wink. "You must miss Boston a good deal."

"I've found it very interesting here," she said.

"I'm glad you said interesting and not delightful or quaint." He gave Donald a friendly glance. "You have an honest wife here, Donald. And let me tell you, honesty is unusual in a female. Because of the lack of it, our patron Saint Columba banished them from his island retreat."

"Nonsense," Glenna protested. "All Scotsmen have an eye for the lassies!"

Laura's eyes met hers. "I've heard this is a great place for romance."

Glenna smiled mockingly. "I'm glad you're so well informed. And about that Sunday we invited you to dinner and you couldn't come. It was just as well. I was called away by the illness of my sister in Sydney and I had no time to let you know."

Glenna moved on to greet Austin. Laura felt relieved! So that explained it!

It was the beginning of an evening in which Laura was to see her husband in a different light. He was suddenly in a much more amiable mood than she'd expected and he paid a great deal of attention to the redheaded enchantress. In fact, several times she felt ashamed that he neglected her to cater to the arrogant Glenna. David MacGregor did not create the same attention as his attractive wife but remained quietly in the background talking with several of the older men most of the evening.

Laura noticed that Anna was in John

Graham's company a good deal of the time when she wasn't busy helping with the party arrangements. Once, when Laura was standing completely alone while her husband and Glenna formed part of a gay laughing circle, Anna gave her a knowing smile across the wide living room.

Aunt Caroline announced the concert and they all gathered to enjoy it. The singers had a varied selection of lively and sentimental Scottish airs and were roundly applauded, but the Presbyterian minister's readings from Robert Burns were the hit of the evening.

In the brief pause after the concert, and before they filed in to the buffet, Laura found herself with David MacGregor, who said, "We're very fond of Donald. He's one of our closest friends."

Laura offered a small smile. "He and your wife seem to get on very well."

He laughed politely. "I say Glenna brings out the best side of him. Donald is a little too serious for his own good. Glenna knows how to take him out of it."

"So it seems."

David MacGregor looked worried. "You mustn't take the wrong meaning from their friendship," he said. "I know many do. But I'm Glenna's husband so I think I may speak with some authority. It has never been a source of worry to me."

Laura privately wondered if the obviously weak David MacGregor would dare object about anything his wife might take it in her head to do. She said, "I'll try to keep that in mind."

"Please do," he urged. Donald has had trouble enough. I say he is entitled to some happiness. And he is lucky to have a wife like you."

It was late in the evening when Frank Cameron arrived at the party, making his entrance through one of the rear doors so as not to cause comment by his lateness. He was wearing the army dress uniform that Aunt Caroline had requested, and when he advanced with a smile to greet Laura, she thought he had never looked better. In fact, she realized he had all the Cameron charm and it was only his affliction that made him seem so different.

He took her hand. "My apologies to the guest of honor," he said.

"I wondered if you were coming."

He sighed. "June isn't well tonight. It was the earliest I felt like leaving her."

Laura was touched by his solicitude for his wife in contrast to Donald's neglect of her all evening. "I'm sure Aunt Caroline and everyone else understands," she assured him. "And now you must try to enjoy yourself."

"I will," he promised. Glancing across where Donald and Glenna were still in conversation, he added, "I see Glenna has your husband in her clutches. Suppose I begin by rescuing him."

"You needn't be the martyr," she demurred.

Frank laughed. "No trace of the martyr in me. Glenna is a pretty girl. I'll have fun." He went across and spoke to Glenna.

It was only a few minutes later that Donald came back to Laura rather shame-faced. He was flushed and his eyes were bright with excitement. "It's turned into a fine party, hasn't it?" he said.

"I'd say that Glenna made it a success for you," she ventured coolly.

He looked startled. "Why pick on Glenna?"

"I'm not," she said. "I'm merely stating a fact. You've been with her most of the evening."

"We're supposed to mingle with our guests!"

"Mingle," she said. "Not monopolize."

He scowled, saying, "I didn't know you

were given to jealousy. I must say it isn't very becoming."

She forced a smile. "Call it something closer to disgust," she said, and walked away from him.

The party was at its height and she moved from one group of guests to another, wanting to give herself a chance to recover her temper by indulging in polite social exchanges with the guests.

As she made the rounds, she came face to face with John Graham, standing with a drink in his hand. Smiling, he said, "Well, I'd say a certain young woman has learned something about her husband tonight."

"Meaning what?" she asked, pretending not to understand what was so bitterly painful to her.

"There's always a bright side," Graham said in his joking fashion. "Once you have your freedom, I'll be able to speak my mind."

"Don't count on the opportunity," she said, turning from him. There were times when John Graham's sense of humor verged on the cruel and this, she felt, was one of them.

Aunt Caroline announced the buffet and they all went in to serve themselves from the long tables with their fine silver and china. Candles in tall silver candelabra cast a flickering light on the heaping dishes of food. Turkey, ham and roast beef formed the solid entrees of a feast which offered Mrs. Basset's kitchen magic at its best. There was praise for the buffet from all sides.

Afterwards Laura drifted to a group around Aunt Caroline. She was talking about the coming Highland Festival, and seeing Laura, she smiled and said, "My dear, you must show them the costume you're making for yourself." To the other guests she confided, "She is using the costume on a Highland doll given her by her husband as a pattern."

Everyone in the circle showed polite interest. Laura tried to avoid discussing it but Aunt Caroline persisted, saying, "Go up and get the doll. It's a little beauty. I want you to show it to them."

Rather than make a scene, she finally agreed, hurrying up the stairs, feeling that it was a silly errand, and wishing that the party would come to an end quickly. Donald had spoiled it for her.

Making her way down the corridor, she opened the door of her room. Switching on the light, she went directly over to the dresser where she kept the doll. She saw that it had fallen on its side and picked it up. As she did so she issued a startled gasp and her eyes blurred with tears. Someone had twisted a bit of cord around the doll's neck and severed its head!

CHAPTER ELEVEN

Remembering it all afterwards, the balance of that Saturday evening seemed like a nightmare to her. Somehow she had made an appearance downstairs again, offering an excuse for not finding the Highland doll. But her mind was filled, to the exclusion of everything else going on around her, with the vision of the hapless doll with its head neatly severed. Of course it had been done as a mocking warning to her.

Laura glanced across the room where Donald was saying goodnight to the Mac-Gregors and paying special attention to Glenna. Need she any longer doubt that her husband had some dangerous streak of insanity in him? A mad side to his nature which he had successfully concealed until after their marriage. Was there any point in trying to protect and believe in him any longer?

"You look ill. Is anything wrong?" It was Donald's brother who had come up beside her to anxiously put the question to her.

She turned to Frank Cameron. "I had a

shock just now. Something upstairs."

"Is there anything I can do?"

"Nothing. It's not anything you should be concerned about. Someone played a malicious trick on me."

Frank looked dismayed. "Have you told Donald?"

She gave a bitter little smile. "I haven't been able to get him alone long enough."

Frank glanced toward the main entrance, where the guests were filing out. "The MacGregors have gone now, so he should be available," he said. As soon as Frank left, Laura went over to Aunt Caroline, and after congratulating her on the party and thanking her, excused herself on the honest grounds of having a severe headache. This allowed her to hurry upstairs before any of the others. She noted the questioning expression on Aunt Caroline's thin face as she quickly left her, but was in no mood to worry about what she might think.

She was too filled with despair and confusion. Going straight to her room, she rushed through her routine of preparing for bed and was under the covers with her eyes shut before Donald entered the room. He came over to the bedside and called her name but she pretended to be asleep. She heard him walk away and quite a few minutes later he turned off the light and joined her in bed, leaning over to gently touch his lips to her cheek.

Her eyes filled with tears but she did not acknowledge the gesture. The incident of the decapitated doll and his flirting with Glenna had marred the evening for her. The business of the doll had renewed all her terror of living in the old castle.

It was true that Glenna had cleared up one troubling point when she had mentioned being unexpectedly called away that Sunday by her cousin's illness. It bore out the story Donald had told of their invitation. It was also quite believable that Glenna's husband had been drinking and by the time she had phoned had been too incoherent to bother giving any proper reply, beyond the abrupt words that his wife was away. Laura saw it as another case in which she had been too quick to pronounce her husband guilty. Unless, of course, Glenna had lied to back up his story.

Long after she heard his easy breathing, as he fell into a sound sleep, she lay awake nagged by doubts and fear. Perhaps Donald had acted no worse than many other husbands. In spite of his attentions to Glenna, he might be completely faithful to her. But there was the shadow that still hung over them all because of Fiona's unsolved murder. Donald should be doubly discreet because of this, but he wasn't!

When she awoke, Donald had dressed and left. Downstairs Mrs. Basset told her he had gone riding. "The party was a grand affair now, wasn't it?" Mrs. Basset said.

"I'm sure everyone enjoyed it," Laura said, smiling at her from the table. "And your food was the main attraction."

Mrs. Basset laughed happily. "I can't say that I'm sorry it's over. It was a lot of work. And now it will only be a little while until we have the big Highland Festival here. Cameron Castle is surely alive again!"

After breakfast Laura decided on a stroll across the broad front lawn, hoping it might clear her head. She still felt miserable and so far had not been able to reach any decisions about what she should do. She knew there was no use asking anyone else for advice. This was something she must settle for herself.

It was a lovely June morning and she felt warm enough, even though she was wearing a rather light print dress. She passed the flagpole with its Union Jack flying proudly and went on as far as the gravel roadway. She was walking along it at a slow pace, her head bent in thought, when she heard the sound of a horse coming near and glanced up quickly to see Donald approaching on a graceful roan. In a moment he was close to her. He reined the horse, swung down from the saddle, and came over, leading the horse.

"I've wanted to talk to you," he said seriously.

"Please, not this morning," she begged, looking away.

"I'm sorry if you think I misbehaved last night," he apologized. "I was caught up in the spirit of the party. It seemed the first carefree couple of hours I'd had in ages."

"Let's not rehash it all," Laura said, keeping her eyes averted.

"And I want to know about the doll," he went on. "What happened to it? Did you destroy it in a rage?"

She turned to him now, anger in her wide blue eyes. "I did not! I think you are the one responsible!"

He was incredulous. "Why would I do such a mad thing? I gave you that doll. It meant something to me. I was shocked to see it mutilated."

Laura stared at him, wavering as to whether to believe him or not. Again he was playing his role convincingly if this was all a pretense. She had been let down so badly before, she felt she dared not listen to him.

"I can't stand living in this place," she said in a low, despairing voice. "From the time we arrived here our relationship changed. You changed!"

"What kind of talk is that?" He frowned. "Because I was friendly with Glenna last night, you want to make a lot of it. I've known her for a long while. It's a perfectly innocent friendship."

"So her husband informed me," Laura said bitterly.

"David knows," he agreed. "I should think that might have satisfied you. If I neglected you during the evening, I apologize and promise it won't happen again."

"It shouldn't have happened last night."

"The MacGregors hadn't been our guests in ages," he argued. "I know the way some of the people gossip and pick on Glenna. I was trying to protect her and see that she had a good time."

"And instead you succeeded in placing both yourself and her in a bad light."

He stared at her in confused silence a

moment. "If I did that, I'm sorry," he said. "It wasn't my intention either to hurt you or make us the center of attention. I wanted just the opposite."

"Well, that's what you managed to do," she accused him. Her eyes searched him sorrowfully. "I don't understand you, you've changed since we were married."

"You've a wild imagination," he said. "You're allowing it to run away with you."

She shook her head. "No! I still love you. That's my weakness. But I can't close my mind to what has happened here and forget your behavior with Glenna last night. There are still the attacks on me to be explained. And the decapitated doll!"

"I told you last night. I've been trying to get to the bottom of things, to find out who it was who came in and attacked you the other night."

"What have you actually done about it?" she demanded crisply.

His face was deathly pale. "I've made some headway. I'd rather not go into the details until I'm more certain."

"That sounds suspiciously like an alibi," she retorted. "As far as I know you haven't done a single thing. I'm beginning to wonder if you really want to."

"You can't believe that," he argued.

"Give me a little time."

"If you really loved me, you'd take me away from this grim old place with its ghosts, hatreds and danger!"

He stared at her in silent frustration as she wheeled around and walked away. She was heading along the road to Frank's cottage and didn't look back. Not until she'd gone some distance did she realize she didn't want to see Frank or his invalid wife in her present state, so she turned and went back to the towering grimness of Cameron Castle. She went upstairs to their room and when she opened the door, Donald was standing there waiting for her.

"I hoped you'd come back soon," he said. "I must finish explaining to you."

"No need," she said wearily.

"Be fair to yourself as well as me," he said. "I know how you feel about the castle and I don't blame you. I haven't done much to help."

"We've gone into all that." She tried to avoid his eyes.

He moved slightly so she could still see his concerned face. "I know we've come to the crisis of all this," he admitted. "So I'm going to make you an offer. The Highland Festival takes place in two weeks. If things haven't cleared up by then, I promise to take you away from here. I'll go wherever you say."

"What right have you to keep me here even another night?"

"None, I suppose," he admitted. "But I do have responsibility for the Festival. As head of the Cameron Clan it is my duty to be here and oversee things."

"And what about your responsibility to me?"

"I hope to fulfill that as well."

She looked at him, not quite ready to believe him. "You make it sound such a small request. You ask me to live on here in terror for another two weeks, to try and pretend I'm not frightened. It's too much to expect!"

He was silent for a moment. Then he said, "Perhaps you're right. But I can see no other way. So I ask it in the name of our love."

Closing her eyes wearily, she said, "You're blackmailing me! Using our love to force me to do this."

"All right," he said. "I'll even admit to that. Just give me the time I need."

She looked into his tense, weary face and thought it was in startling contrast to the carefree mask he had worn at the party. There was little of the gallant who had paid court to the redhaired Glenna in his manner now. Which of the two was the real Donald Cameron? Was he some mad combination of these opposite types, his brain twisted by the struggles of his opposing natures. And would she be signing her own death warrant by showing a willingness to remain in the eerie old castle for the extra weeks he had requested.

Laura hesitated, then said, "Because I have to give you every chance, I'll stay. I know I may be making a mistake that will cost me my life. But I married you and love you. If this is what you want, then I'll go along with it."

It was settled between them, and Laura prepared to face the ordeal of another two weeks in the house. As the days passed, the weather grew warmer and everyone at the castle became involved in the preparations for the Highland Festival in the same way they had for the party, but this outdoor celebration was being planned on a community scale.

The fact that it was being held on the Cameron grounds made their front lawn a scene of humming activity the week before the gathering. Lumber was trucked in, and overnight various stands and booths were erected near the flagpole. When the bare structures stood finished, the workmen set out to deck them with multi-colored canvas and turn them into attractive settings for the various activities. At suitable spots, great lines of flags were stretched from building to building, and electricians moved in with rubber cables and outdoor electrical plants to provide a fairyland pattern of lights for the event.

Laura saw little of her husband. She counted off the days, while constantly living in fear of this man she had loved. She tried to hide this from the others, but wondered if she'd really managed to deceive them. Every day she walked with Aunt Caroline to watch the workmen at their preparations. The old woman never seemed to tire of visiting the site and telling any of the workers who took a moment to listen of the glory of the old time fairs.

Austin Cameron no longer made any reference to the night of her attack, even when they were alone, but she still sensed an awkwardness in the professor's manner toward her. Anna was coolly friendly and nothing more, and Laura noticed that she and John Graham were spending almost all their free time in each other's company.

She wondered if a romance was developing. She thought they might be well suited and hoped that if it did turn out that way they would be happier than she and Donald.

Posters showing pipers against a background of a sunny scene of Highland games were put up all over the area, and at last the morning of the big day arrived. It marked a special milestone for Laura because of her bargain with Donald that they would leave the castle as soon as the Festival had ended. So far he had done nothing to clear up the mystery of the attack on her, and with no progress made at this late date, she felt it was an admission of defeat on his part. So, they would go. And yet, even in the face of all her fears, she would somehow be sad now in leaving.

But Highland Games Day was not one for moping. Under Aunt Caroline's stalwart direction, Laura and Anna were the proprietors of a booth selling homemade fudge prepared by Mrs. Basset. The proceeds from the candy were to go to a fund for a boys' Rugby team. By eleven in the morning a steady parade of cars and trucks were depositing people on the grounds, and what a colorful group of people! Kilts were the order of the day, and pipers were as thick as the dandelions poking up through the green grass.

It was an intriguing show of colorful pageantry; a peep show of tartans, and strong men wrestling with timbers the size of telegraph poles to the drone and fury of massed pipe bands. These burly contenders, staggering under the burden of 'cabers,' while running, leaping and jumping, were the chosen athletes from many towns and villages. Elsewhere, young girls mounted the platform to dance in kilts, with their blouse fronts adorned with medals. Laura learned that day that piping was of two kinds: the swaggering music of a full band with pipes, drums and drum major, and the music of the solo player.

It was this solo piping that touched her heart, that made her ponder on the unhappiness that had come between her and the man she loved. She listened to the sad, sweetly wailing strains and thought how much it told of the Scotch way of life and the Scotch heart.

Anna, who was standing beside her in the candy booth, was pensive and was also plainly moved by the piper's sad air. When he finished, she looked at Laura and said, "There are maybe a dozen on the whole island who can be truly termed 'pipers' and he's one of them. He plays what we call in Gaelic *ceol mor* — the big music, *piobaireachd* — and the tune he was playing is about our own Cameron Castle and what happened here so long ago, the 'Sheila MacLeod Lament.' It's part of local folklore now."

"I can understand that," Laura said quietly, glancing beyond the carnival scene and crowds at the towering, gray stone castle in the background. Perhaps Aunt Caroline was right. It had known dark terror from that first murder in its beginning and the shadow had descended on the Camerons down through the years. She and Donald were the latest victims.

There was no time to indulge long in such thoughts. The crowd continued to grow, and she and Anna were besieged by adults as well as children. Mrs. Basset's homemade candy was popular with old and young alike and they had few idle moments. Donald came over to tell her that all attendance records had been broken, and he seemed in one of his best moods. She wondered if he remembered their agreement, and whether he hoped she would not hold him to it. She would remind him of her decision to leave as soon as this Festival day had ended.

By late afternoon the lawn was a mass of people, and the games were coming to an exciting conclusion. John Graham came over to make a small purchase and stood talking for a moment. He wore his usual smile of secret amusement. Laura thought how different he was in disposition from her husband, even though the two men looked so much alike. But then, Donald and Frank were the very opposites in nature and appearance even though they were blood brothers.

Graham interrupted her reverie by saying, "A friend of yours has just arrived." He glanced across at a booth where prizes were being offered for those successfully throwing hoops over mounted prongs of colored wood.

She followed his glance to see Glenna MacGregor standing there. Wearing a tight, dark green dress and with a small white dog on a plaid leash, Glenna was apparently trading jokes with the proprietor of the game, while the dog strained to move on.

"I like her little dog," was Laura's comment.

"That's Whiskey," Graham told her. "It's a West Highland Terrier, one of the standard Scotch breeds. Most people think of them as white scotties but they are a separate and distinct breed. Glenna thinks more of Whiskey than she does of David." He turned to her again, a teasing gleam in his eyes. "Maybe even more than she does of Donald."

Laura met his look unflinchingly. "Has anyone ever told you you're much too sarcastic to keep friends?'"

He regarded her with mock dismay. "Surely you're not angry with me?"

Anna who had been busy with customers joined them. "Angry with you? Why should she be?" she asked.

"It isn't important!" Laura said, her cheeks flushing.

"We were just admiring Glenna and her dog," Graham explained. Glancing across the way again, he said, "She seems to have moved on."

Laura couldn't help wondering if Donald had met Glenna and if they were now having the same gay time together they had had on the night of the party. Her thoughts were answered when she left the booth to have lunch in the big tent that had been set up for serving meals.

Aunt Caroline was one of those selling tickets at the entrance, and when she saw

Laura, she looked suddenly uneasy. Laura didn't understand why until she went inside and sat at one of the tables to be served. Donald and Glenna were there, sitting side by side, talking earnestly. They didn't see her, so intent were they on whatever they were discussing, and she had the impression that they might even be arguing.

Laura hoped they wouldn't see her since they were seated at the other end of the tent. The big rush was over and she sat at a table with no one else near her. From time to time she glanced in their direction and saw when Glenna stood up to leave. She had brought the small dog into the tent with her, which was most likely an infraction of the rules, but Laura didn't suppose that would present much of a problem to her. Glenna was used to breaking all sorts of rules.

She left by the opening at the other end of the tent, so she did not pass near Laura. Donald sat down again to finish his tea, and Laura concluded that they had not entered the tent together but had arranged to meet there. She returned to her own meal and tried to put the whole business out of her mind.

She succeeded so well that she didn't

notice Donald as he came up to her. Seating himself in a vacant place on the bench beside her, he smiled and said, "I didn't see you come in."

She gave him a knowing glance. "You were probably too preoccupied."

At once he understood. "You saw me talking to Glenna."

"I saw you together," she corrected him.

"We weren't together," he said. "I made up my mind you'd have nothing to complain about today. We just happened to meet in here."

"You seemed to have something very serious to discuss."

He frowned. "Maybe we did. I've been wanting to ask her several important questions. I think I found out something just now that may interest you."

Laura was inclined to think he was bluffing again, pretending to have had some important business with Glenna in order to placate her. "It doesn't matter to me anymore."

"Let's not start that again," he pleaded.

"I mean it," she said, rising to leave.

He stood up with her, his handsome face indignant. "I don't mind being treated this way when I'm in the wrong, but I resent it when I'm not. You're not being too fair yourself now."

Laura gave him a scathing look and hurried out. It was easy to lose herself in the crowd and she had no idea whether he tried to follow her. She felt a little ashamed of her own attitude. On this festive day she might at least have pretended to have more good will towards him, but seeing him talking so intimately with Glenna had angered her. Slightly dismayed, she wondered if she hadn't been just plain jealous. Was she still that much in love with him?

When she returned to the booth, Anna regarded their depleted stock of candy and informed her, "Mrs. Basset has nothing more to give us. I think you can clean up the little that is left and then shut down the booth. I'd like to take the rest of the evening off."

"By all means." Laura smiled. She had an idea that Anna wanted to join John Graham for some of the fun and dancing that would follow later.

She was surprised when half an hour later she saw Donald and Anna strolling arm in arm. They were talking and laughing and looking completely at ease. As they moved on toward the other end of the lawn, where the bandstand was set up, Laura found herself feeling forlorn and left out of things. A very small amount of candy was left but sales had slowed down. The focus of interest had turned to the bandstand where flaming torches had been fixed to the posts to create an old-fashioned atmosphere. With dusk settling, the band was now playing lively jigs, and some square dancing had already started.

She had about made up her mind to close the booth anyway when Frank came along. He was wearing his Highland army uniform again and he greeted her with a warm smile.

"I see they've found you a job and kept you at it," he said.

"I'm considering deserting my post any minute now," she told him.

He laughed. "But think of the disappointed face of some child who arrives here with coins in his grubby little fingers, all ready for a treat, and finds you gone."

"That grubby-fingered little child had better come soon then," she said, laughing. Then she asked the usual question. "How is June?"

Frank sighed as he glanced toward the bandstand. "You know how it is when she feels she's missing something. I'm afraid she was pretty depressed when I left her. But I felt I had to put in at least a belated appearance with the Festival being held on the estate. We Camerons have always tried to live up to our responsibilities."

"It's been a wonderful success according to Donald," she said.

His brother nodded. "I imagine he stood with the mayor while all the speeches were being read. They always thank us for the use of the grounds each year, but I haven't noticed them sending anyone to help clean up after they've taken their stuff away."

Laura smiled. "Human nature! By the way, Glenna MacGregor is here."

"Really? I haven't seen her," Frank said. "I hope she isn't making a scene of herself with Donald again."

She shrugged. "They were in the dining tent together. He claimed they just happened to meet."

Frank looked disgusted. "I have heard those stories before," he said. "I suppose I must go on and mingle with the crowd. I'll look for you later."

"I'll keep an eye out for you," she promised. It was dark now and the music filled the air as Frank strolled off toward the platform where a lively square dance was under way. The tiny multi-colored electric lights that lined the booths had come on to add their magic to the night, and the blazing torches flickered against the dark sky.

She suddenly had an unexpected run of luck and the last of the candy was disposed of in a few minutes. Collecting the money, she turned the lights out on the stand and left the comparatively deserted aisle of booths to join the others. The first person she met was Anna Gordon.

She was alone and came up to Laura, a worried look on her face.

"So you sold out," she said.

"Yes. I thought I'd go up by the bandstand for a while and watch the dancing."

"You should," Anna agreed. "Donald is there somewhere." She gave Laura a searching look. "What have you been saying to him?"

"We've barely talked. Why do you ask?"

"He was in a depressed mood when I met him. I tried to cheer him up."

"I saw you strolling past the booth. You seemed to be making out well," Laura said with a wry smile.

"Donald can only take so much," Anna warned her. "You should show more understanding. Don't blame him if he turns to Glenna tonight." With this rather unexpected warning Anna went on her way.

Frowning to herself, Laura continued toward the grandstand and the crowds around it, but when she reached the fringe of the happy throng she caught no glimpse of Donald, or even of Glenna. Feeling more depressed each minute, and deciding she was in no way participating, she began to think of going across to the castle and up to bed.

She was turning to leave when she saw the little white dog running toward her, trailing its leash. Glenna's dog! Whiskey came up to her, staring at her with his solemn little face, and made a whimpering sound. She at once felt sympathetic toward the shaggy fellow and bent down to pat him. He responded but seemed nervous and unhappy. Laura found it hard to reconcile Graham's story of Glenna's great love for the little dog with the fact that she'd allowed him to run loose among the crowds this way. Anything could happen to him! For no reason she could understand, she felt a sudden, chilling fear surge through her. She took his leash and went on saying a few comforting words to the obviously distressed dog.

Straightening up, she strained to see if she could catch a glimpse of Whiskey's mistress but none of the faces around her were familiar. With the little fellow tugging at his leash, she began to walk round the outside of the crowd as the gay jig continued. She was still looking for Glenna when she ran into Donald a few minutes later.

His face was lined and weary. Donald stared at the dog and then at her in complete amazement. "What are you doing with Whiskey?" he asked.

"I found him running loose," she said.

"Glenna must have lost him somehow," he said, glancing around. "We'll have to try and find her. She'll be frantic."

Laura was about to answer when the scream came. It came from the bushes near the cliff. It was female, loud and piercing, and could be heard even above the dance music. Startled faces turned in the direction from which the cry of terror had come, and as the screams continued and drew gradually nearer the festival grounds, the band stopped playing.

She turned with the others and stared as a couple appeared out of the night. The youth had his arm around the shoulders of the girl who was staggering forward, her head bent and sobbing hysterically. The young man's face was strained.

"It's Glenna MacGregor," he announced in a taut voice for all to hear. "She's behind the bushes! Murdered!"

Donald was nearest the couple and took

a step toward them, his face deathly pale. "What are you saying?" he demanded.

"Glenna has been murdered! Strangled! There's a cord or something around her neck," the boy said. Donald turned to Laura and she was terrified by what she saw in his face.

CHAPTER TWELVE

A hush fell over the merrymaking as the full meaning of the young man's words was understood by the crowd. Then came the reaction. Troubled murmurings filled the air; parents quickly sought out children who had strayed; they stared at each other white-faced, in stunned amazement; and they phrased over and over again in different words what had happened. The Mounted Police, who had been in attendance at the Highland Games, quickly took charge.

It was inevitable that the mass of people should drift near the spot where Glenna's body had been found and stand in awe as the grim tragedy continued to unfold. The Mounted Police arranged for a powerful spotlight to be moved from the fair grounds to the place where the murdered woman still lay.

A montage of these moments would always remain in Laura's mind: the tense expression on her husband's face as he left her to join the Mounties in investigating the scene and in helping to keep order; the blank despair on the face of David Mac-Gregor as he stood, a privileged and solitary figure, within the area blocked off by the police, absently holding the leash of Glenna's little dog, which Laura had turned over to him.

Two men with angry frowns on their faces stood on her right. She didn't know them, nor did they appear to recognize her. Watching the police at work one of them said, "Donald Cameron is making himself mighty busy!"

The other jeered. "Maybe he's making sure of getting himself in the good graces of the police again. They let him off last time. Didn't even charge him and I'd be willing to bet he murdered that Sutherland girl."

"So now they've got a second killing on their hands," the first man went on. "And he acts like he was the big noise! Glenna probably was pushing him for money, so he got rid of her. According to that kid, she was killed the same way Fiona was!"

Laura could listen to no more of it. Feeling she might faint, she turned and slowly walked back to the now almost deserted lawn. Then she saw a familiar figure coming to meet her and she felt better at once. It was Frank Cameron.

Frank's face was grim. "I've been looking all over for you. I know how you must feel," he said, putting an arm around her.

She leaned against him and found some small comfort in realizing she at least had him to turn to. She whispered, "What do you think?"

"I don't dare think!"

"I saw them together earlier tonight. In the dining tent."

Frank nodded. "You told me about it."

"They were arguing." Her voice faltered. "But I can't believe he killed her!"

"Thanks!" The voice was dry and familiar, and she wheeled with a gasp to see Donald studying her grimly, his face ashen.

"Donald!" she said, going to him.

It was his turn to hold her off this time. He took her by the hands and turned to his brother. "This is going to be a bad night here. I know how she feels about this place and everything else. Can you take her home with you?"

Frank was quick to answer. "Of course. We have plenty of room."

"No!" Laura protested, looking up into her husband's stricken face. "I won't leave. It isn't fair."

"I want you to go," he said in a way that

allowed no argument.

"But what will happen to you?" she asked.

"I'll be all right," he assured her. "You go upstairs and pack what you'll need for the night."

Her eyes were wide with fear. She whispered, "Will you be suspected? Is there any chance of your being involved in this?"

"They're not liable to forget about Fiona," he said grimly. "Anything can happen. You'll be better with Frank."

"Get your things," Frank told her. "I'll be at the front door with the car in ten minutes."

When she had gotten a nightgown and a few other necessary extras in a small bag and hurried down the dimly lighted stairs to the door, he was standing on the steps waiting. She could tell at once that he was upset and eager to get under way.

"I'm glad you're on time," he said, leading her down to the car and helping her in. He put her bag in the back seat and got behind the wheel. "It's a nasty business," he said.

As they reached the main highway a Mountie on patrol halted them and Frank explained who they were. The policeman let them drive on. Then Laura turned to him and asked, "What did you find out?"

"The sergeant in charge was questioning Donald when I left," Frank said, frowning. "I'm afraid they'll give him a lot more attention as a suspect this time."

"I heard people in the crowd practically saying he was guilty," Laura said in despair. "And mentioning Fiona's murder as well."

Frank nodded. "They're almost bound to connect the two murders, and even though Donald is my brother and your husband, I have to face the fact that he is the most logical suspect."

"I suppose so," Laura said sinking back against the car seat with a hopeless feeling. She was already beginning to wish that she had stayed to see it through. Even though Donald might be a murderer, she was still his wife and she loved him. In spite of his insistence that she leave the castle for the night, she now began to wish that she had remained, but Frank had also urged her to come with him.

"I don't know who else it could be," Frank worried.

"Perhaps someone who knew both girls as well as Donald and looks enough like him to be mistaken for him."

Frank gave her a swift glance. "There is

only one person answers that description. John Graham!"

"I know," she said wearily. "And I can't see any way to connect him with either killing."

"I'm too rattled to think clearly yet," Frank said. "Perhaps we'll be able to cope with it better in the morning."

"I hope so," she said, although she felt it was just talk on their part. They both were convinced that Donald was a double murderer and only reluctant to put their opinion in words.

Frank brought the car to a halt beside the cottage. He turned to her and said, "June will be asleep. Better not to wake her now. I'll be talking to her in the morning. She wakes up very early. I'll tell her then. It won't be as terrible as hearing it now."

"Of course," she agreed, but she doubted that June would be too surprised, or that she'd worry any about what happened to Donald. From the beginning she had openly accused him of being a murderer.

Frank saw her quietly into the house and assigned her to a small, attractive bedroom. She prepared for bed, but between the strange surroundings and her distraught frame of mind, she had no more than one or two half-hour periods of broken sleep. As soon as she heard Frank up in the morning, she got out of bed. By the time she had washed and dressed she could hear his deep voice and June's thin, whining tones in conversation in June's bedroom, although she couldn't tell what they were saying. All the while she was being nagged by a growing sense of shame. She had been wrong in running away from the horror at the castle the previous night. She should have stayed, even though Donald had insisted she leave.

When she finally left her room and joined Frank at his wife's bedside, June greeted her by saying, "You poor creature! I knew this would happen! I've always said what that husband of yours was. Now what are you going to do?"

Laura drew herself up very straight. "I'm going back to him as soon as Frank will take me."

June appeared astonished. "You don't really mean it?"

"I do. It was good of you and Frank to take me in last night. But I know I shouldn't have come."

"I'm sorry, Laura," Frank mumbled. "Perhaps I was too quick in trying to persuade you. I hoped I was doing what was best."

"I understand," she said. "And I appreciate it."

"I think you're being a little fool," June said tartly. "The next thing you know he'll murder you!"

"Please, dear!" Frank wheeled on his wife with the first angry words Laura had ever heard him direct at her. And in a more moderate tone he went on, "Whatever you may think, Donald is my brother!"

They left the room soon after that, and when Laura had finished breakfast and packed her bag, she said good-bye to June and started back to the castle. Frank drove slowly and seemed deep in thought.

At last he said, "I've been thinking about what you said. And it could be that John Graham is deeper in this than he'd like to have us guess."

"He has a strange disposition," she agreed. "But I don't know."

"Naturally one doesn't want to accuse anybody hastily," he said. "But Graham should be regarded as a suspect. We shouldn't just assume that Donald is the guilty party."

"Perhaps the police have already done that," she said gloomily.

It was a dark, cloudy Sunday morning with a hint of storm. A wind had come up and as they drove close to the castle, the grounds provided a dismal sight. Only a few things had been taken down and the grass was scattered with litter. Down by the bushes a Mounted Police car was parked and she saw a policeman seated in it. The castle seemed quite deserted as they drove up to the main entrance, but just as they were getting out of the car Anna appeared in the front doorway. Laura guessed she was probably starting on a walk.

The girl gave her a condescending look. "So you've decided to come back?"

Frank took a position on the steps between them and said, "You shouldn't take that tone to Laura. She's been through a good deal."

Anna smiled coldly. "At least she missed most of last night."

"I'll admit I shouldn't have left," Laura said frankly. "What happened? How is Donald?"

"He was up most of the night," Anna said. "Right now he's in the village at Mounted Police Headquarters."

"Then they've charged him with Glenna's murder?" Frank said.

Anna shook her head. "They hadn't up until the time he left here." Anger glinted in her eyes as she regarded Frank. "And you ought to be the last one to suggest they should! I didn't see you here standing up for him last night either!"

"I did what I felt was best," Frank said in an unhappy tone.

Anna shrugged and walked on down the steps and away from them. Frank saw Laura inside where Mrs. Basset informed them that Aunt Caroline was in a state of shock. Frank at once went up to her room while Laura continued to her own room, worrying about Donald and wondering what might be happening at police headquarters.

Laura was so completely absorbed in her thoughts that she did not see Austin standing on the landing until she was almost on top of him. She stared at him with startled eyes.

"You gave me a start," she said.

He nodded. "I'm sorry. I didn't intend to. Actually I came up to see if you'd returned."

"Frank just drove me back."

"It's a dreadful business," he said with an embarrassed glance her way. "I still think we should have notified the police the other night. Then this might not have happened."

"I wonder."

Austin glanced down the stairs almost comically to make certain no one was within earshot. Then he leaned toward her and asked, "Do you think Donald murdered her?"

"Why should I?"

"Almost everyone does. Even Aunt Caroline," Austin went on nervously. "I don't know what to think. Both Fiona and that Glenna were frivolous young women. Donald seems to have a liking for females of easy character." He realized what he'd said and at once added, "Not meaning you, of course."

"I understand," she said wearily. "Why should my husband murder Glenna?"

"I don't know! Maybe they had some kind of quarrel. I hear she had a bad temper."

"I wonder if a lot of what we hear isn't pure gossip," Laura said bitterly. "Even the part about her character. A girl with Glenna's spirit is apt to cause talk in a small town, even though she may be perfectly innocent of any wrongdoing. Her husband went out of his way to explain that to me the night of the party, and I should have listened to him. She was young and pretty and loved her little dog."

Austin Cameron stared at her in amazement. "You sound as if you were defending the girl?"

"I think probably I am," she said in a quiet voice, "although I must admit it's a little late for it." She went on to her room, leaving Austin staring after her, amazed and troubled.

Somehow Austin's conspiratorial air had made her angry. For a moment his smugness seemed to represent that of all the people in this small village. They were all too quick to pass judgment on those whose actions they didn't properly understand, and perhaps she was as much to blame as any of them. Anna had been right. She shouldn't have left last night.

She remained in her room the balance of the day. It continued dark and forbidding, as if the very elements were affected by the tragedy. Mrs. Basset came up with a tray of sandwiches and tea for her at dinner time. The housekeeper was in a depressed mood. She informed Laura that Frank had persuaded Aunt Caroline to take a sedative before he left, and she was still sleeping.

"You should take something too," she suggested.

Laura, standing by the window, waiting for Donald's car, said, "No. I don't want to sleep. I'm hoping my husband will be back soon."

Mrs. Basset's round face was wrinkled with worry. "Poor Mr. Donald! What a terrible thing to have happen here on Festival night. I expect we'll never have one again without remembering that poor woman."

Laura nodded. "She is apt to be remembered as long as Sheila MacLeod. The castle will have a new ghost."

"Isn't it true," Mrs. Basset said in an awed tone as she went on her way.

Laura ate one of the sandwiches and had a cup of tea. Then she resumed her vigil at the window. Just as dusk was settling, her heart gave a bound. Donald's car appeared in the drive. She wanted to race down the stairs and greet him, but somehow she couldn't; not with her feeling of shame.

She waited. She was standing in the middle of the room when he opened the door. She could tell by his hopeless expression that it had not been a good day for him.

He stared at her for a long moment in silence. "You're back," he said at last.

"Yes. I'm back."

"You shouldn't have left Frank's place." His voice was cold.

"Donald, I was wrong. I freely admit it!

Wrong all last evening," she said. "I shouldn't have been jealous of you and poor Glenna. I'm sorry. And I was wrong to allow you and Frank to persuade me to leave here."

"It struck me as what you really wanted to do," he told her.

Laura's eyes blurred with tears. "I'm here to stay. Whatever happens."

"Thanks. I wish that would solve all our problems, but it won't."

"How badly are you involved? Will they charge you?"

He nodded. "I think so. I've been warned not to leave here. I'd say they'll press formal charges tomorrow."

She swallowed hard. "It will pass the same as before. Then we can go away."

His eyes burned into hers. "Let's not pretend anymore."

"I love you," she said, and came toward him with open arms.

"Too late for that," he said sharply, and before she could reach him, he turned quickly and let himself out of the room, slamming the door. She heard his footsteps pounding down the stairs and gazed blankly at the closed door.

A roll of thunder broke the silence in the room, thunder loud and close at hand.

Then there was a sharp flash of lightning. She turned and went over to the window as a cloudburst of rain suddenly descended. With her eyes fixed on the roadway in front of the house, she saw Donald stride out and head around to the back of the castle in the pouring rain. He wore neither hat nor raincoat and seemed not to notice the storm at all.

She was filled with an overwhelming need to reach him somehow and explain. A few minutes ago she had tried and failed, but too much was at stake to let it go at that. In the mood he was in, she couldn't allow him to wander out there alone in the rain. She must make a further effort. She quickly found her raincoat, threw it over her shoulders, and hurried down the stairs. The thunder and lightning were coming at regular intervals now. A blinding flash halted her momentarily on the second landing, then she rushed down the rest of the way. Deciding she could best reach him by the back door, Laura went down the long, dark hallway and out the rear door. She stood in the shelter of the doorway a moment, and when the lightning flashed again, peered out into the darkness. She could see no sign of him in the yard.

Then, as the night and rain closed in on

her again, she suddenly knew where he must have gone. The tired phrase burned in her mind like a special message: "A murderer always returns to the scene of his crime!" It hit her with a stunning impact. He had gone back to that deserted spot where Glenna's body had been found. She knew what she must do. She had deserted him last night; she would stand by him now.

Without hesitating, she braced herself against the storm and made her way across the lawn. The lightning flashed again, revealing the macabre shapes of the canvas-covered booths standing like ghostly sentinels, flapping in the wind and driven by the rain. She circled the festival area, thinking only of Donald and what quirk of madness had pushed him to such lengths.

Now she was close to the scene of the tragedy. The police car had gone. There was no need to keep a man posted here in such a storm. She stumbled on through the wet grass, drenched even though she had her raincoat for protection. Her whole body trembled as a great clap of thunder seemed to burst directly above her. And then the lightning came and she saw him standing there before the bushes. In the vivid blue light she could not mistake his features.

"Donald!" she cried through the storm and ran toward him.

This time he responded, coming to her with outstretched arms. She felt a small relief until the lightning flashed briefly again and she saw the cord he was holding. Too late! As the cord slipped over her head and was roughly tightened around her throat, her bewildered eyes gazed at his face distorted by a mad smile of assurance.

"No! No!" she begged for mercy.

Her body twisted in his arms so that her back was to him, and now the cord was cutting off her breath. She gasped and as a peal of thunder ended, the lightning flashed again and she saw a figure advancing. She was so close to losing consciousness that she doubted her eyes, for the figure she saw in that moment was Donald's.

Through glazed eyes she saw Donald come nearer. At the same time she realized the cord had slackened around her throat, and she was sliding down on the wet grass. She dimly heard Donald cry out and then she lost consciousness.

She was in her own bed, in her own

room, when she opened her eyes. Donald was seated by her, a worried expression on his face. "Thank Heavens! I was afraid you were never coming to!"

She raised herself up on one elbow, her alarm returning.

"Where is he? What happened?"

He pressed her gently back on the pillow. "Lots of time for that. How are you?"

"I'm all right," she said. It was a gross exaggeration, for her throat was paining again in a familiar way. The cord had almost done its job.

"I'll believe that after the doctor arrives and has a look at you," he said. She now noted that he was dripping wet, his curly hair streaked flat against his forehead. There were still drops of water at his temples and on his cheeks.

She said, "I went out to the bushes to find you."

"A crazy thing to do," he told her. "It's lucky I happened to see you crossing the lawn and followed."

Laura crossed a hand wearily over her eyes and then stared at him. "There were two of you," she said.

"That's the trouble," he said. "There has been all along. My double almost finished you tonight as he did Fiona and Glenna."

"He slipped the cord around my throat," she said, fear crossing her face as she recalled it. She stared up at her husband. "And then you came."

"It was touch and go," he said. "And he put up quite a battle."

Her eyes were wide. "Who was it?" she asked tautly. "Who is the murderer?"

"I'm surprised you haven't guessed. Who looks almost exactly like me? So much so that with a little makeup he's been able to fool everyone."

"John Graham!"

He shook his head. "A good guess. Graham does look a lot like me but he isn't the murderer. In fact, he's downstairs now guarding the murderer until the police arrive."

"If it wasn't Graham I don't know," she said wearily.

"And yet you know him so well," her husband said sadly. "I don't blame you. I never would have guessed either."

"Who?"

"Frank."

"Frank!" Disbelief showed in her face.

"I grant you I didn't know who it was until I knocked off the wig he was wearing. A wig that exactly matched my hair. Then I saw that he had painted on eyebrows and used false lashes to complete his disguise. Add them all up with his facial structure so basically like mine and you have my double."

"Not Frank!" she whispered. "I trusted him so! I admired him."

"So did everyone else." Donald's expression was grave. "That was what made it so easy for him. No one guessed."

"But why did he kill her? And Fiona."

"His motives were sound enough," Donald said grimly. "For a beginning he had been carrying on an affair with Fiona Sutherland for some time. Fiona felt guilty being June's best friend and wanted to break it up. Frank resented it and arranged a meeting with her one night when he was disguised as me. He killed her. He hoped to blame it on me. But one person saw through his game. Glenna! She worked in the same building with him and saw him enter his office as me and leave as himself. This put her on to his game and she began blackmailing him."

"And she never let on to you?"

"No. But she made several teasing remarks that mystified me. Not until yesterday did I begin to guess she must be blackmailing someone. I talked to her about it. That's what was happening when you saw us together in the dining tent."

"But she didn't tell you anything?"

"She as much as admitted it but wouldn't give me any names. I told her it was a dangerous business." He sighed. "I didn't know just how dangerous, or how close she was to paying for it."

"So he killed her here on the grounds last night, again intending to throw the suspicion on you."

"Yes. That rid him of any threat she offered and left only you to stand in his way."

"Stand in his way?"

"Of taking over as the heir to the castle. With you and me out of the way he could settle down to run the estate. It's what he's always wanted, and I think he's had his eye on Anna."

"And of course he had Aunt Caroline fooled completely," she said.

"Poor old girl! It will be hard on her!"

"I believed it was you," she said, sitting up in bed. "I was attacked by someone who looked like you almost as soon as I got here. And he came after me again the night you were in Halifax. It was Frank who Austin saw on the stairs."

Her husband nodded. "He wanted your testimony on record that I'd tried to kill you before he finished the job. He knew you had told Graham and Austin and they would talk after you'd been discovered murdered. He found out some way that the police were going to charge me tomorrow and lock me up. So he had to finish you tonight while I was still around to take the blame. He was certain your murder would tie up all the loose ends and clear his path to take over here."

Laura looked rueful. "And I did all I could to help him by going out there in the storm like a ninny."

He frowned. "He would have come for you anyway, if you'd waited. Likely he was planning to come later; make his way in by one of the side doors and finish you up here." He paused. "Just what did make you go out there where Glenna was killed anyway?"

She stared down at the coverlet, embarrassed. "I was trying to follow you. I had no idea where you'd taken off to. And then I remembered that thing about a murderer always going back to the scene of his crime."

He raised his eyebrows. "It wasn't such a bad idea. Only you had the wrong person in mind as the criminal."

Laura stared at him in awe. "It did work

out, didn't it? He was the murderer and he was standing down there. It gives me cold chills."

"Old sayings usually have a lot of truth in them," he said with a sigh. "The police should be here soon. There'll be June to see and tell. Aunt Caroline to cope with. And the family will have to bear the scandal of it. It won't be easy."

She touched his arm gently. "We'll manage somehow."

"We?" His eyes opened wide. "I thought you had enough of Cape Breton. That you wanted to get away from here as soon as possible."

"Don't be ridiculous!" she exclaimed. "I love this country in spite of all that has happened."

"Then you must love it very much indeed," he agreed.

"And you!" She stretched out her arms. This time he did not turn away from her, and they shared a kiss that was long and meaningful. Laura was almost serene in the comforting protection of his arms. Indeed they were so lost in their moment of bliss that they did not hear the door open, or see Anna come in until she gave a small warning cough.

She said, "I've been taught to knock. But

I don't as a rule."

Donald was on his feet facing Anna quickly. "I didn't hear you," he said, his face flushed. "What is it?"

"The police are here," Anna said. "They want to see you before they take Frank away."

"I'll go down," he promised. Turning to Laura, he said, "I'll be back as quickly as I can. The doctor should be here soon."

"Don't worry about me," she said.

Donald crossed to the door, and rather awkwardly told Anna, "Laura and I . . . we . . . ." His voice trailed off.

Anna nodded. "You don't have to explain," she said. "I understand perfectly."

Donald hesitated only another moment before he went out, leaving them alone in the room. Laura felt a wave of affection for the lovely girl standing by the door.

She said, "It seems I'm to find happiness here after all. I hope it will be the same for you."

Anna surprised her with a sudden shy smile. "And why not? Your own love has made you blind to what's been going on around you. John Graham has asked me to marry him — and I've accepted."

"That is wonderful news," Laura

exclaimed, smiling warmly at Anna. And, she thought, what a perfect climax to a day that had begun with such doubt and terror. It promised happier times ahead at Cameron Castle.

1	31	61	91	121	151	181	211	241	271	301	331
2	32	62	92	122	152	182	212	242	272	302	332
3	33	63	93	123	153	183	213	243	273	303	333
4	34	64	94	124	154	184	214	244	274	304	334
5	35	65	95	125	155	185	215	245	275	305	335
6	36	66	96	126	156	186	216	246	276	306	336
7	37	67	97	127	157	187	217	247	277	307	337
8	38	68	98	128	158	188	218	248	278	308	338
9	39	69	99	129	159	189	219	249	279	309	339
10	40	70	100	130	160	190	220	250	280	310	340
11	41	71	101	131	161	191	221	251	281	311	341
12	42	72	102	132	162	192	222	252	282	312	342
13	43	73	103	133	163	193	223	253	283	313	343
14	44	74	104	134	164	194	224	254	284	314	344
15	45	75	105	135	165	195	225	255	285	315	345
16	46	76	106	136	166	196	226	256	286	316	346
17	47	77	107	137	167	197	227	257	287	317	347
18	48	78	108	138	168	198	228	258	288	318	348
19	49	79	109	139	169	199	229	259	289	319	349
20	50	80	110	140	170	200	230	260	290	320	350
21	51	81	111	141	171	201	231	261	291	321	351
22	52	82	112	142	172	202	232	262	292	322	352
23	53	83	113	143	173	203	233	263	293	323	353
24	54	84	114	144	174	204	234	264	294	324	354
25	55	85	115	145	175	205	235	265	295	325	355
26	56	86	116	146	176	206	236	266	296	326	356
27	57	87	117	147	177	207	237	267	297	327	357
28	58	88	118	148	178	208	238	268	298	328	358
29	59	89	119	149	179	209	239	269	299	329	359
30	60	90	120	150	180	210	240	270	300	330	360